Developing
FRENCH

PHOTOCOPIABLE LANGUAGE ACTIVITIES
FOR BEGINNERS

Livre Deux

Madeleine Bender

A & C BLACK

**early
language learning**

"Developing French is a photocopiable resource in three books that provides opportunities for enjoyable mixed-skills activities to children beginning French in Key Stage 2, following the content of the QCA Guidelines and Scheme of Work. Extensive teachers' notes, accessible to non-specialist teachers and parents, are supplemented by access to online pronunciation support for pupils and teachers. A full-colour classroom frieze with relevant vocabulary is included in each book, as are details of further resources."

ELL is a DfES initiative managed by CILT, working in partnership with QCA, BECTa, the British Council, the TTA, Ofsted and the Association for Language Learning.

Reprinted 2003, 2006, 2007
Published 2002 by A & C Black Publishers Limited
38 Soho Square, London W1D 3HB
www.acblack.com

ISBN 978-0-7136-6295-5

Produced for A & C Black by Bender Richardson White, Uxbridge

Project editor: Lionel Bender
Text editor: Lucy Poddington
Designer: Ben White
Page make-up: Malcolm Smythe
Production: Kim Richardson

The publishers and author would like to thank the headteacher, staff and pupils of Iver Heath Junior School, Buckinghamshire, for their help and assistance in developing and testing the activities.

A CIP catalogue record for this book is available from the British Library.

Printed in Great Britain by Caligraving Ltd, Thetford, Norfolk.

A & C Black uses paper produced with elemental chlorine-free pulp, harvested from managed, sustainable forests.

Contents

Introduction

Developing French supports the teaching of French to beginners. It is designed for teachers and parents with French-language skills of any level. The books contain teaching ideas and photocopiable activities which develop children's abilities to communicate in French and to appreciate French culture, customs and traditions. The activities provide opportunities for listening, speaking, reading, writing and comprehension. They will encourage children to enjoy learning the language and to feel confident about trying to speak French whenever they visit France or a French-speaking country or meet French people.

This series follows closely the Qualifications and Curriculum Authority (QCA) guidelines and scheme of work for teaching Modern Foreign Languages (MFL) in primary, middle and special schools at Key Stage 2. The books can also be used to support the teaching of French at Key Stage 3 for pupils who have had no prior teaching of the French language.

The activities in **Developing French** help children of all ages to:

- become familiar with the sounds and written form of a modern foreign language
- develop language skills and language-learning skills
- understand and communicate in a new language
- increase their cultural awareness by learning about different countries and their people
- be confident and competent in listening, reading, speaking and writing in a foreign language.

Teaching requirements

The teaching and learning activities in **Developing French** are designed to be carried out in classroom lessons or at after-school clubs. They can also be used at home. The children will benefit most if all teaching is in French, but this is by no means essential. The books can be used by a non-native speaker with at least GCE or GCSE French, or secondary school French.

Pronunciation guide

When you speak French to the children, it is important that your pronunciation is as accurate as possible. A basic pronunciation guide is provided on page 8. An on-line spoken pronunciation guide linked to this book, which can be used by both teachers and pupils, is available on the A & C Black website at www.acblack.com/developingfrench

If your French needs refreshing, it's a good idea to reacquaint yourself with the language by listening to French-language tapes or CDs, watching French films or French television and using French websites. On page 62 there is a list of recommended books and websites.

Developing French Livre Deux

This book covers mainly the middle group of units of the QCA MFL scheme of work, focusing on the following aspects of everyday life:

- parts of the body
- items of clothing
- shops and shopping
- food and drink
- where people live
- counting up to 1 million
- transport
- countries and flags of the world.

For the best results, give pupils a daily 10-minute French lesson or two 20- to 30-minute lessons each week. If this is not possible, use opportunities such as meal times, registration, games and assemblies to introduce and practise French.

Encourage the children to practise language learnt in French lessons at other times: for example, when greeting each other in corridors or when doing household jobs at home.

If you are a confident French-speaker, conduct all your lessons in French. If you are a little unsure of your French skills, using some English will make things easier and less contrived. It can also be helpful to act out situations and use mime with the children.

The book is divided into five topics. At the start of each topic are two introductory pages which provide:

● key vocabulary with translations

● grammar points

● learning objectives

● teaching ideas to introduce the topic

● notes on how to use the activity sheets

● further activities.

Key vocabulary

Each topic begins with a list of important words and phrases that are used in the activities. Where appropriate, it is indicated which words and phrases the children should learn, which are for recognition only, and which are for revision.

While faultless pronunciation is not essential, you should ensure that a clear distinction is made between such words as *un* and *une*, and *le, la* and *les*. Also be aware of instances where a mistake in pronunciation sounds like a grammatical error, such as when it is necessary to sound the final consonant of an adjective to make it into its feminine form (for example, *petit/petite*).

Teaching ideas

Also at the start of each topic there are suggestions for ways to present the new language to the pupils and to use it in a daily context or as introductions to the activity sheets.

The teaching ideas include ways of integrating French into the general school day as well as into French lessons.

Photocopiable activity sheets

These are intended to support your teaching, not to replace it. They incorporate exercises and strategies that encourage independent learning: for example, ways in which children can evaluate their own work or that of a partner.

The activities use a range of questions, puzzles, quizzes, comprehension tests and games to reinforce and extend the children's learning of French and provide opportunities for you to assess their progress. Most of the sheets are for the pupils to use individually, but some involve paired work. Some of the sheets can be used to create playing cards and flashcards for revision activities and games. These sheets will benefit from being enlarged on a photocopier before being given to the children.

The activity sheets are illustrated, where possible or relevant, with French objects, situations and scenes. We have used as the main characters a French boy and girl, Pierre and Marie. They appear throughout the book. We also introduce a number of Pierre and Marie's friends and relatives, to help children identify with French people.

Instructions and text Ensure that the children are familiar with the new vocabulary and grammar before they try out the activity sheets. All the instructions and text on the activity sheets are in French. At the start of each instruction is an icon to aid understanding. Exposing children to as much French as possible helps them to understand and communicate in the language. Translations of all headings and instructions are given at the bottom of each activity sheet.

Word banks On many of the activity sheets there is a vocabulary list (*Liste*) from which the children may choose their answers. For some activities the children will need a French–English dictionary, but it is a good idea to make one available to them at all times to reinforce vocabulary work.

Extension activities Most of the activity sheets end with a challenge (*Et maintenant* – literally 'And now'). These challenges might be appropriate for only a few children; the whole class should not be expected to complete them. Some pages provide space for the children to complete the extension activities, but for others they will need a notebook or separate sheet of paper.

Teachers' notes At the foot of each activity sheet are teachers' notes, which include:

- translation of the instructions for the main activity and, following a bullet point (•), for the extension activity
- the learning objective
- a summary of the vocabulary and language skills children will need to practise before using the sheet
- advice on how to use the activity sheet in the classroom or at home.

These footnotes can be masked, if you wish, when photocopying the sheets.

Suggestions are also given for introducing the activity sheets to the children. Choose the way that you feel confident with and best suits the pupils' abilities. If possible, mime how to complete the activity sheet while reading the French instructions and pointing to the relevant parts of the sheet.

Or explain in English what the instructions mean. If you are teaching younger children or those requiring more support, you could fill in for them the first letter or word of the answers.

Differentiation Most of the activity sheets can be used in more than one way. Various possibilities are suggested, as well as ways of specifically adapting exercises to differentiate the work. Children requiring support could work in pairs.

For best results, suggest that the children fill in the sheets using a pencil rather than a pen, so that they can rub out any mistakes and not spoil the look of the finished sheet. Pupils can put their finished sheets into a folder to keep for reference.

Picture dictionaries

These illustrated spreads can be photocopied and used as revision aids. If enlarged and laminated, they can be displayed on the classroom wall. Here are some possible revision and display uses:

- make the pages the focus of a finding game: ask questions such as *Où est le chat?* or *Où sont Marie et Pierre?* The children can answer orally or point to the correct part of the picture.

- for vocabulary revision, mask or cut off the vignettes and labels around the edges and ask the children to write the French names for as many things in the illustration as they can.

- for revision of *un* or *une*, *le* or *la*, mask or cut off the border area and give each child a copy of the picture dictionary and ask them to colour in specific items that you name in French (tell them which colours to use). Or, using two different colours, they can colour-code the masculine and feminine nouns in the picture.

- for more able children, ask them to write the French names of items they can identify in the main illustration that are not shown in the dictionary around the border.

Recommended resources

On page 62 there are details of French language teaching and learning materials that you may find useful to refer to. Some will help you to brush up your language skills. Others are suitable for the pupils to investigate. Other helpful teaching resources are traditional French nursery rhymes and poems related to the topic you are teaching. Tapes and books of them are available in specialist bookshops. You will find more detailed and extensive French-language teaching plans in the QCA Modern Foreign Languages Teacher's Guide and in numerous publications from the Centre for Information on Language Teaching and Research (CILT).

Answers

You will find answers to all the questions, wordsearches and crosswords on pages 63 and 64.

Pull-out frieze

Inside the back cover of the book is a giant pull-out frieze. This can be used as the centrepiece of a permanent display in the school or classroom. The children could look in French magazines and holiday brochures for pictures to cut out and display around the frieze, such as French food, landmarks or celebrities.

Ideas for games and role-play

These work well with group or whole-class learning situations. The following ideas can be used with any topic and at any time – they can be performed as extensions to, or separate from, the activities on the photocopiable worksheets. The games can be made to last between 5 and 15 minutes, depending on the time available and how well the children respond.

Stand up/sit down game

Ask the children to stand in a circle (or at their desks if you prefer) and ask them questions in turn. If the first child gives the correct answer, he or she remains standing. If the child does not know or gives an incorrect answer, he or she should sit down in the middle of the circle (or in their seat) and you ask the same question to the next child. Continue until a correct answer is given. At this point, the children sitting down can be invited to repeat the correct answer, to include them in the rest of the game. The game can be ended at any convenient time, when one child or several children remain.

Instant reward game

This game works best if the children are sitting down on a large carpet or in the middle of the classroom. Ask questions or show visual aids for vocabulary recognition and invite volunteers to give you the correct information. Give out a reward for every correct answer (make sure the answer is completely accurate – if not, move on to another child). For rewards, use a set of reward tokens or maths interlocking cubes, or simply write points next to the children's names on your class list. Count these up at the end of the game (in French of course!). The child with the most rewards is the winner for the day/week/term.

Le pendu (Hangman)

Play this as you would play English 'Hangman' but with French words and letters called out in French. This is a good activity for learning or revising the alphabet in French.

Jacques a dit (Simon says)

Play this as you would play the game in English, but replace 'Simon says' with *Jacques a dit*. Use actions such as *levez-vous* (stand up), *asseyez-vous* (sit down), *montrez la porte* (point to the door) and mimes such as *nager* (to swim), *jouer au football* (to play football), and *dessiner* (to draw).

Question/réponse

This activity lets the children practise conversation. You say the French word *Question!* and invite a child to ask a question he or she has learnt. When you say *Réponse!* any child can answer. You could write a question mark on the board and point to it every time you say *Question!* Alternatively, show a flashcard of the word.

Pronunciation guide

This page offers guidance on how to pronounce certain letters or combinations of letters in French. For each sound, an English word containing a similar sound is given. Depending on UK regional accents, use alternative sample words. Try out the sounds by reading the practice words aloud several times. It is important to use this guide in conjunction with listening to native speakers, since many of the English equivalents are approximations.

If possible, ask a French-language teacher to help you, or use the online pronunciation guide that accompanies this book on website address www.acblack.com/developingfrench

a, à	like the 'a' sound in 'rat' **practice words:** *la, chat, va, table, avion*
â	like the 'a' sound in 'car' **practice words:** *gâteau, pâtes*
e	like the 'a' sound in 'above' **practice words:** *regarde, le, cheval*
é	like the 'ay' sound in 'late' **practice words:** *écoute, réponse, légumes*
è, ê, ai	like the 'ay' sound in 'say' **practice words:** *règle, frère, être, tête, père, j'ai, chaise*
i	like the 'i' sound in 'twig' **practice words:** *lit, dix, rideau, piscine*
o,	like the 'o' sound in 'pot' **practice words:** *homme, gomme*
ô, eau, au	like the sound 'o' in 'core' **practice words:** *hôtel, beau, jaune*
u	no English equivalent but shape mouth tightly as if to say the 'aw' in 'paw' but make an 'ee' sound **practice words:** *tu, une, du, sur*
an	like the 'an' sound in 'can't' **practice words:** *dans, manger, tante, blanc*
eu	like the 'i' sound in 'sir' **practice words:** *neuf, meubles;* close mouth more for *deux, bleu*
in, ain, im	like the 'an' sound in 'sang' **practice words:** *lapin, vingt, train, pain, main, imperméable*
oi	like the 'wa' sound in 'wag' **practice words:** *trois, oiseau, poisson, toilette*
on	like the 'on' sound in 'long' **practice words:** *maison, oncle, cochon, marron*
ou	like the 'oo' sound in 'good' **practice words:** *douze, sous, mouton, boucherie*
un	like the 'an' sound in 'pant' **practice words:** *brun, lundi, un*
c	like 'k' when followed by a, o , u or a consonant except h **practice words:** *canapé, cochon, cuisine, crayon, école* like 's' when followed by e or i **practice words:** *c'est, cinq, ce*
ç	the same sound as 's' **practice words:** *ça, garçon*
ch	the same sound as 'sh' **practice words:** *douche, cochon, vache, chaise*
g	like the 'g' sound in 'good' when followed by a, o, u, l, m or r **practice words:** *gare, gomme, glace, gris, garage* like the 's' sound in 'pleasure' when followed by e, i or y **practice words:** *genou, gîte*
gn	like the 'ni' sound in 'onion' **practice words:** *araignée*
h	silent **practice words:** *histoire, hôtel, homme*
j	like the 's' sound in 'pleasure' **practice words:** *jambe, jeudi, jupe, jeu, déjeuner*
qu	like the 'c' sound in 'cat' **practice words:** *quatre, chaque, casquette, banque*
r	like a gentle dog growl **practice words:** *robe, rideau, trois, bras, rue, règle*
th	like the 't' sound in 'take' **practice words:** *thé, bibliothèque*

Topic 1: Le corps

Key vocabulary and grammar

For revision:

Ça va?	How are you?

Vocabulary to be used by the children:

la tête	the head
le corps	the body
les bras (un bras)	the arms (an arm)
les jambes (une jambe)	the legs (a leg)
les mains (une main)	the hands (a hand)
les pieds (un pied)	the feet (a foot)
les épaules (une épaule)	the shoulders (a shoulder)
les genoux (un genou)	the knees (a knee)
la bouche	the mouth
le nez	the nose
les yeux (un œil)	the eyes (an eye)
les oreilles (une oreille)	the ears (an ear)
J'ai mal à la tête	I have a headache
J'ai mal à l'oreille	I have earache/my ear hurts
J'ai mal aux oreilles	I have earache/my ears hurt
J'ai mal au pied	My foot hurts
J'ai mal aux pieds	My feet hurt
J'ai mal à l'œil	My eye hurts
J'ai mal aux yeux	My eyes hurt

Song (Head, Shoulders, Knees and Toes):

Tête, épaules, genoux, pieds,
Genoux, pieds,
Tête, épaules, genoux, pieds,
Genoux, pieds,
Et yeux, et bouche, et oreilles, et nez,
Tête, épaules, genoux, pieds,
Genoux, pieds.

Grammar to be used by the children:

• irregular plurals: bras/bras; genou/genoux; œil/yeux

• The verb avoir (to have):

j'ai	I have
tu as	you have
il/elle a	he/she has
nous avons	we have
vous avez	you have
(polite/plural)	
ils/elles ont	they have

For recognition only:

Bis	Repeat (in song)
Aïe! Ouille!	Ouch!
Levez…	Raise…
Baissez…	Lower…
Ouvrez…	Open…
Fermez…	Close…
Touchez…	Touch…
Qu'est-ce que c'est?	What is it?

Teaching ideas

Names for parts of the body

Introduce the vocabulary for parts of the body by saying each word as you point to or touch the relevant part of your body. Alternatively, you could use a volunteer from the class. Make sure that it is absolutely clear which part you are indicating, especially in the case of arms and legs (move your hand along the whole length of the arm or the leg as you say the words *un bras* and *une jambe*). An enlarged copy of the illustration on page 11 could also be used to introduce and/or test the vocabulary.

It is a good idea to introduce the new vocabulary in two stages. For example, you could do the main parts of the body in one lesson and details of the head on another occasion.

For parts of the body which come in pairs, such as arms and shoulders, introduce the plural first and then the singular form immediately afterwards, (*les bras*, *un bras*; *les épaules*, *une épaule*). This is a good opportunity to revise regular and irregular plurals. For regular plurals, simply add an *s*. If the word already ends in *s* in the singular, there is no change for the plural, for example *un bras/les bras*. Most words ending in *u* take an *x* instead of an *s*, for example *un genou/les genoux* (exceptions to this rule can be explained much later). Irregular plurals should be learnt individually as the children come across them.

Sing a song

The French version of the song 'Head, Shoulders, Knees and Toes' (see key vocabulary and grammar) is a fun way to reinforce the vocabulary. Stress that it is not exactly the same as the English version (for example, 'toes' is replaced with *pieds* and the facial features come in a different order).

Simon says

Practise the vocabulary with a game of *Jacques a dit* (Simon says). Ask the children to raise, lower, open, close or touch various parts of the body, for example: *Levez un bras! Levez les mains! Baissez les mains! Fermez les yeux! Ouvrez les yeux! Ouvrez la bouche! Touchez la tête!* and so on. Note that the commands are followed by *un/une/les* and the part of the body, whereas in English we would say 'Raise your arm'. You might want to point out that *Fermez la bouche!* is not rude in any way.

Mime an ailment

Ailments can be introduced using actions and goes down well with children: mime an expression of pain on your face as you say *J'ai mal à la/au/aux* (followed by a part of the body). At the same time, hold or touch the relevant part of the body.

Once the children have learnt how to express ailments, use the question *Ça va?* to prompt a negative response, for example *Non, j'ai mal à la tête.*

Classroom routine

When the children write the date in their French exercise books or on the activity sheets, ask them to use the short numerical form rather than using English words (until you have taught them how to write the date in French). Also explain that French children put their surname first and their 'first' name second on their school work, and that their names are called out in that way when calling the register.

Further activities

Page 12 Practising parts of the body These cards can be enlarged, glued on to card and used for quick-fire vocabulary practice. Hold up a card and ask *Qu'est-ce que c'est?* Alternatively, let the children make their own sets of flashcards, then ask questions which they can answer by holding up the correct card. The children could make extra sets of cards showing the French words for the parts of the body pictured on the cards. They can then use these with the unlabelled picture cards to play matching pairs games, Snap and Pelmanism.

Page 12 Playing *Loto* (bingo) Divide the class into two teams. Cut the sheet in half horizontally to make two *Loto* cards (you could glue these on to card or laminate them). Give a *Loto* card and six counters to each team. Then call out the French names of the body parts on the cards, one at a time. The players in each team confer and place a counter on the correct picture if they have it. When a team covers all their pictures, they should call out *Loto*. Check their card in case they have made a mistake. For additional points they could be asked to say the names of all the items on their card.

Page 15 Dice game Each child should cut their figure along the dotted lines to make six cards. The children in the group put all their pieces together on a table. The aim of the game is to make up a complete body by collecting the cards in sequence: head (1), body (2), left [as viewed by the child] arm (3), right arm (4), left leg (5) and right leg (6). The children take turns to roll two dice and match the dice numbers to the cards. They can use the numbers on the individual dice or add them together, for example, if 1 and 2 are rolled, they can be used to collect cards 1 and/or 2, or for card 3. The child must say the French name for each part of the body they collect (the list on the left of the picture can be used as a prompt). The first child to make a complete body, having named all the body parts correctly, is the winner.

Page 16 Revising *avoir* and parts of the body In the main activity, ask the children to write the English translation beneath each sentence. As an extension, the children could draw some mythical beasts or aliens (using their imaginations!) with different numbers of heads, eyes, ears, arms and so on. Encourage them to write sentences about the number of body parts, using those on the activity sheet as models.

Le corps

 Regarde le dessin.

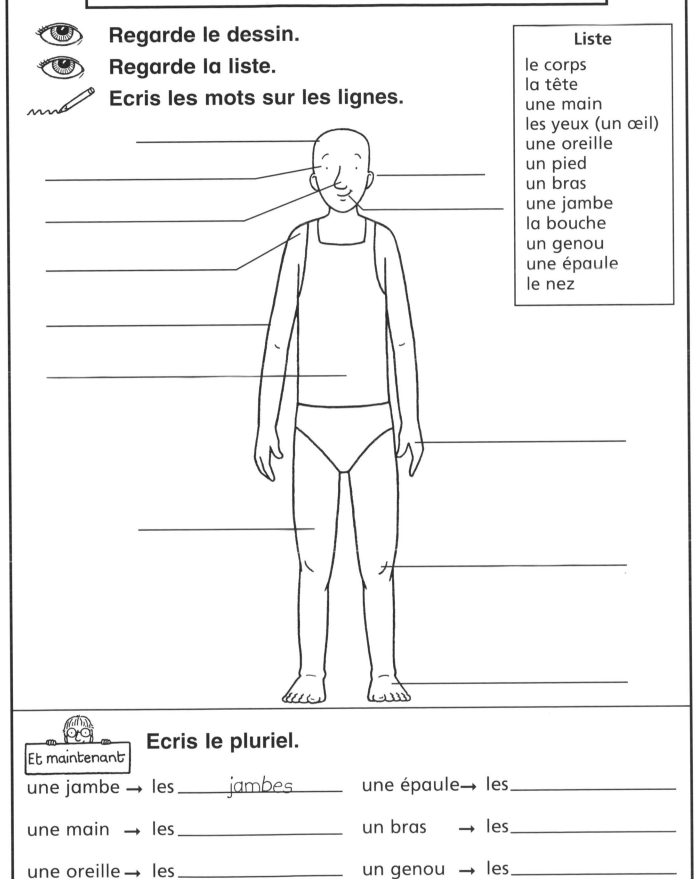

Regarde la liste.

Ecris les mots sur les lignes.

Liste

le corps
la tête
une main
les yeux (un œil)
une oreille
un pied
un bras
une jambe
la bouche
un genou
une épaule
le nez

Et maintenant Ecris le pluriel.

une jambe → les _____jambes_____   une épaule→ les _____

une main → les _____   un bras   → les _____

une oreille → les _____   un genou → les _____

un pied   → les _____

Translation *The body. Look at the drawing. Look at the list. Write the words on the lines.*
• *Write the plural.* **Teachers' note** This activity gives practice in naming parts of the body in
both the singular and the plural forms. Ensure the children are aware that some of the words
are masculine and some feminine.

Developing French
Livre Deux
A & C Black 2002

Les parties du corps

 Regarde la liste.

 Choisis les mots.

 Ecris les mots sous les dessins.

_____ _____ _____

   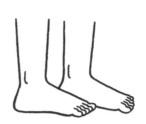   

_____ _____ _____

_____ _____ _____

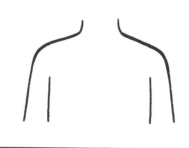      

_____ _____ _____

12

Translation *Parts of the body. Look at the list. Choose the words. Write the words under the pictures.* **Teachers' note** This activity involves practising the names of parts of the body. Once the children have written the answers, they can glue the sheet on to card and cut it up to make flashcards. Alternatively they can use the unlabelled pictures for card games and bingo (see page 10).

Developing French
Livre Deux
A & C Black

Aïe!

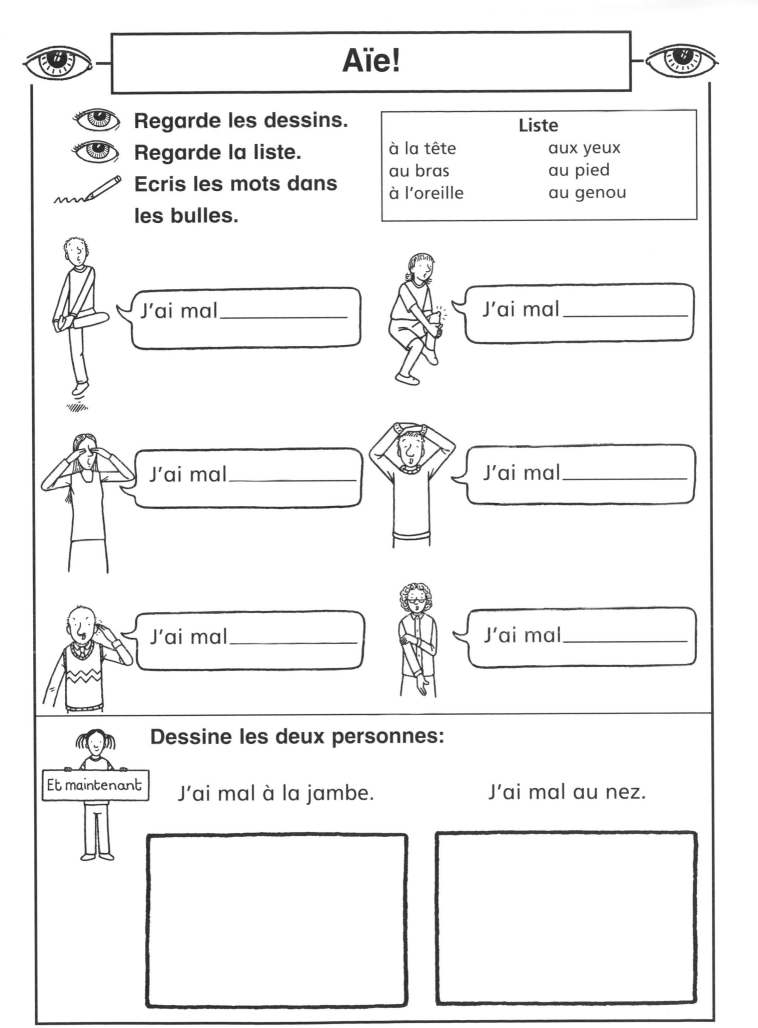

Regarde les dessins.

Regarde la liste.

Ecris les mots dans les bulles.

Liste

à la tête   aux yeux
au bras   au pied
à l'oreille   au genou

J'ai mal_____

J'ai mal_____

J'ai mal_____

J'ai mal_____

J'ai mal_____

J'ai mal_____

Dessine les deux personnes:

Et maintenant

J'ai mal à la jambe.

J'ai mal au nez.

Translation *Ouch! Look at the drawings. Look at the list. Write the words in the bubbles.*
• *Draw the two people.* **Teachers' note** This activity gives practice in naming parts of the body and saying which part of the body hurts.

Developing French
Livre Deux
A & C Black

Méli-mélo

 Regarde les dessins.

Démêle les mots.

Ecris les mots.

Relie les mots et les dessins.

hubcoe _____ •

jebam _____ •

nima _____ •

ungoe _____ •

reellio _____ •

ausleép _____ •

dipe _____ •

olie _____ •

Et maintenant

Démêle les mots. Ecris les mots.

zen _____   sporc _____

Dessine-les.

Dictionnaire

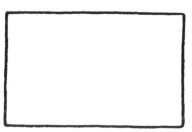

Translation *Mix-up.* Look at the drawings. Unscramble the words. Write the words. Join the words and the pictures. • Unscramble the words. Write the words. Draw them. **Teachers' note** Use this activity to reinforce names of parts of the body and their spelling. Provide the children with a French dictionary so that they can check the spelling of the words.

Developing French
Livre Deux
A & C Black

Jeu de dés

Regarde le dessin.

Regarde la liste.

Relie les mots et les dés.

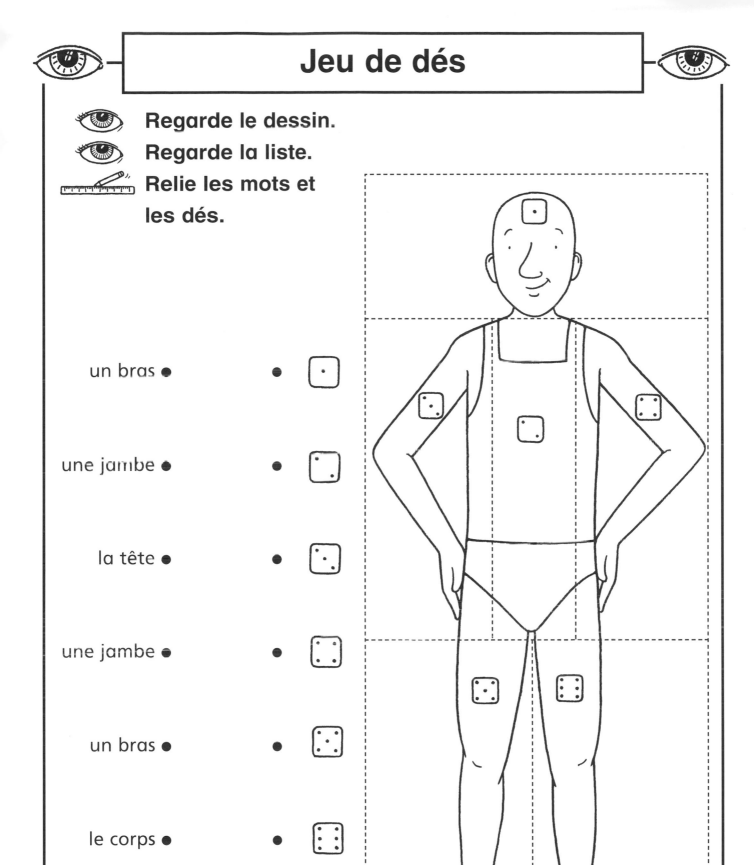

un bras •

une jambe •

la tête •

une jambe •

un bras •

le corps •

Et maintenant **Joue le jeu de dés.**

Translation *Dice game. Look at the drawing. Look at the list. Join the words and the dice.*
• *Play the dice game.* **Teachers' note** This activity gives practice in naming parts of the body.
The children should play the game in groups of three or four. Each group needs two dice, and
each child needs a copy of the sheet (laminated or glued on to card if possible). For details of
how to play, see page 10.

**Developing French
Livre Deux
A & C Black**

Avoir

 Regarde la liste.

 Choisis les mots.

 Complète les phrases.

1. Nous __avons__ deux pieds.

2. J' _____ deux épaules.

3. Nous _____ une tête.

4. Ils _____ deux bras.

5. Il _____ deux yeux.

6. Tu _____ une bouche.

7. Elles _____ un nez.

8. Vous _____ deux oreilles.

9. Elle _____ deux mains.

 **Et maintenant**

Ecris les parties du corps dans les cases.

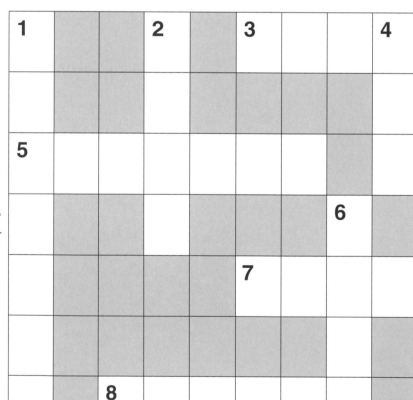

Developing French
Livre Deux
A & C Black

Une chanson

 **Illustre la chanson.**

Dictionnaire

"Tête

Epaules

Genoux   Bis
                (Répète)
Pieds

Genoux

Pieds

Et yeux

Et bouche

Et oreilles

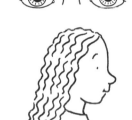

Et nez

Tête

Epaules

Genoux

Pieds

Genoux

Pieds"

Et maintenant   **Ecris la chanson anglaise.**

_____

_____

_____

_____

Translation *A song. Illustrate the song.* • *Write the English version of the song.*
Teachers' note Explain that the children should draw a picture for each line of the song, showing the correct body part. The illustrations on the right-hand side of the page may help them. Explain the word *bis*, meaning 'repeat', and provide dictionaries in case the children have forgotten any words. Sing the song as a class, with the actions, to finish off.

Developing French
Livre Deux
A & C Black

Topic 2: Les vêtements

Key vocabulary and grammar

For revision:

je voudrais	I would like
Donne(z)-moi …	
s'il te/vous plaît	Give me … please

Vocabulary to be used by the children:

une chemise	a shirt
une chemisette	a polo shirt/short-sleeved shirt
un sweatshirt	a sweatshirt
un pullover	a pullover
un pantalon	a pair of trousers
une jupe	a skirt
une robe	a dress
un collant	a pair of tights
des chaussettes (une chaussette)	socks (a sock)
des chaussures (une chaussure)	shoes (a shoe)
une casquette	a cap
un anorak	an anorak
rouge	red
rose	pink
jaune	yellow
orange	orange
beige	beige
bleu	blue
noir	black
vert	green
gris	grey
blanc	white
violet	purple
marron	brown
les cheveux blonds	fair hair
châtain	brown hair
bruns	dark hair
roux	red hair
gris	grey hair
blancs	white hair
les yeux bleus	blue eyes
verts	green eyes
marron	brown eyes
De quelle couleur?	What colour?
De quelle couleur est…?	What colour is…?
Vous désirez?	What would you like?
C'est combien?	How much is it?

numbers 31 to 1000: *trente* (30), *trente et un* (31), *trente-deux* (32), *trente-trois* (33), *trente-quatre* (34), *trente-cinq* (35), *trente-six* (36), *trente-sept* (37), *trente-huit* (38), *trente-neuf* (39), *quarante* (40), *cinquante* (50), *soixante* (60), *soixante-dix* (70), *soixante et onze* (71), *soixante-douze* (72), *soixante-treize* (73), *soixante-quatorze* (74), *soixante-quinze* (75), *soixante-seize* (76), *soixante-dix-sept* (77), *soixante-dix-huit* (78), *soixante-dix-neuf* (79), *quatre-vingts* (80), *quatre-vingt-un* (81), *quatre-vingt-deux* (82), *quatre-vingt-dix* (90), *quatre-vingt-onze* (91), *quatre-vingt-douze* (92), *cent* (100)

Grammar to be used by the children:

• masculine/feminine forms of adjectives: *bleu/bleue; noir/noire; vert/verte; gris/grise; blanc/blanche; violet/violette*

• the verb *porter* (to wear):

je porte	I am wearing/I wear
tu portes	you wear
il/elle porte	he/she wears
(nous portons)	(we wear)
(vous portez)	(you wear) (polite/plural)
ils/elles portent	they wear

Teaching ideas

Names of items of clothing

Using real clothes as visual aids (either your own discarded ones or items from a charity shop) is by far the best way to introduce the vocabulary for items of clothing. Pull items out of a bag one at a time and name each one. Ask the children to repeat the names several times. Once they are familiar with the vocabulary, invite them to ask you for items of clothing: for example, *Donne(z)-moi la robe/le pantalon* or *Je voudrais les chaussettes* (along with *s'il vous plaît* [when asking you] or *s'il te plaît* [when asking another child]. 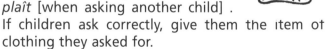 If children ask correctly, give them the item of clothing they asked for.

After this, play a game in which the children ask each other for items of clothing. Distribute the items among the children and choose one child to begin asking. As long as the child does not make a mistake, he or she may carry on asking the others for the clothes. If the child dries up or makes a mistake, the person who was being asked takes over. Whoever has the most clothes at the end of the game wins (the game can end at any time, or when one child has succeeded in collecting all the clothes).

The cards from the activity sheet on page 20 can also be used to introduce or test the new vocabulary.

Introducing colour

Introduce colours initially in their masculine singular form using *Ça c'est rouge, ça c'est vert*, and so on. Teach the colours in the order they appear in the list on the left, as they are grouped according to how they change (or not) in the feminine form.

When the children are confident about their meaning, show them how to put the colour words with nouns. Begin with the first group of colours (which do not change in the feminine form). Explain that the colour adjective always comes after the noun. Then do the same with the remaining colours, introducing the way in which an adjective can change (usually by adding an e) with a feminine noun. Point out that some changes occur in the spelling which do not affect the way the words are pronounced, for example *noir/noire*. Also draw attention to the irregular adjectives, i.e. *blanc/blanche*, *violet/violette*, and *marron* which never changes.

To practise this, make up a large card with 12 pairs of trousers drawn and coloured on one side and 12 dresses on the other (one of each colour). Point to one item and say the phrase, for example, *un pantalon vert*. Then flip the card and point to the item of the same colour on the other side, i.e. *une robe verte*. Go through all the items in turn and stress the changes in pronunciation when they occur.

When the masculine and feminine variations have been practised sufficiently, introduce the plural forms of the adjectives. All colour adjectives except *marron* take an *s* for the plural in both masculine and feminine forms, unless they already end in *s* (i.e. *gris*). Also, explain to the children the French used to describe hair and eye colour.

The verb *porter*

Ask the children to describe what they are wearing using *je porte…* You can also use pictures cut from magazines and catalogues as visual aids. Ask the children to describe what various people in the pictures are wearing, using *il/elle porte…*

Numbers 31 to 100

Teach the children numbers from 31 to 100 so that they can say prices. Once *quarante*, *cinquante* and *soixante* have been introduced, the numbers in between are simple for the children to work out themselves and learn, allowing them to count up to *soixante-neuf* with the addition of only three new words to their vocabulary. They can then take *soixante-dix* to *soixante-dix-neuf* in their stride. Counting on from *quatre-vingts* is at first a bit daunting, but once the children understand that the beginning stays the same up to *quatre-vingt-dix-neuf* they manage quite well. *Cent* comes as a great relief after that!

Further activities

Page 20 Flashcard games These cards can be enlarged, glued on to card and used for quick-fire vocabulary practise. Hold up a card and ask *Qu'est-ce que c'est?* Alternatively, let the children make their own sets of flashcards, then ask questions which they can answer by holding up the correct card. They can use the picture and word cards to play matching pairs games, Snap and Pelmanism.

Page 20 Playing *Loto* (bingo) Divide the class into two teams. Cut the pictures on the sheet into two sets to make two *Loto* cards, each with six pictures (you could glue these on to card or laminate them). Give a *Loto* card and six counters to each team. Play *Loto* according to the instructions on page 10.

Page 24 Practising numbers 40 to 100 The children can use these cards for matching pairs games, Snap and Pelmanism. They could also practise putting the word cards into the correct numerical order.

Page 24 Playing *Loto* (bingo) Divide the class into two teams. Cut the word cards on the sheet into two sets to make two *Loto* cards, each with ten number words (you could glue these on to card or laminate them). Give a *Loto* card and ten counters to each team. Play *Loto* according to the instructions on page 10. The numbers can be read out in English or written on the board in figures. A set of bingo cards showing figures could also be used, with the numbers called out in French.

Les vêtements

 Découpe les cartes.

 Mets les mots avec les dessins.

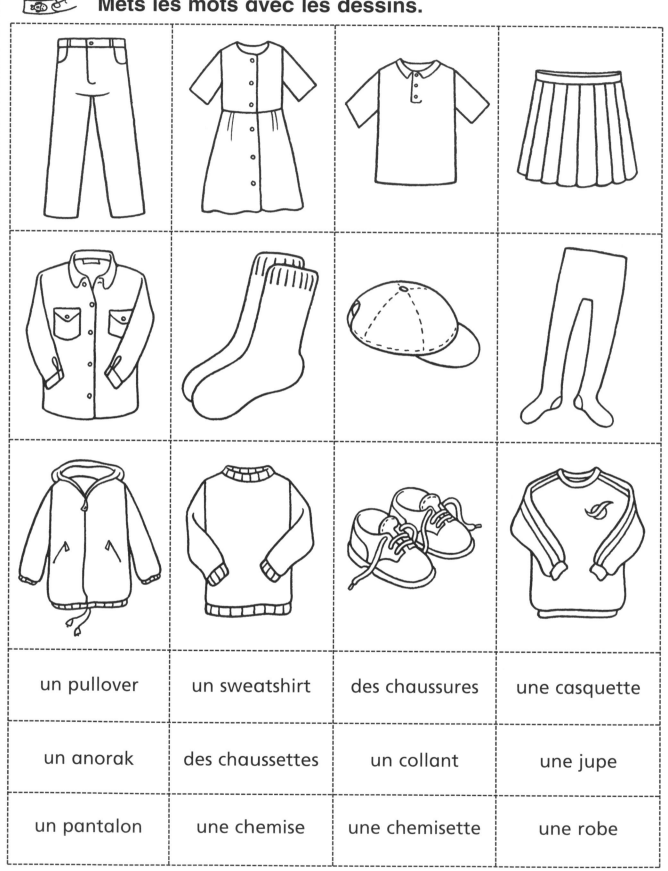

un pullover	un sweatshirt	des chaussures	une casquette
un anorak	des chaussettes	un collant	une jupe
un pantalon	une chemise	une chemisette	une robe

Translation *Clothing. Cut out the cards. Put the words with the drawings.* **Teachers' note** This activity helps the children to learn the names of items of clothing. Once the children have matched the pairs, they could glue the pictures and matching captions on to a large piece of paper. Alternatively, they can glue the whole sheet on to card and cut it up to make flashcards. The cards can be used for card games and bingo (see page 19).

Developing French
Livre Deux
A & C Black

Les couleurs

 Colorie chaque carré de la bonne couleur.

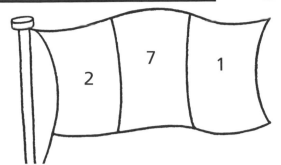

1 rouge		2 bleu		3 jaune		4 vert	
5 rose		6 noir		7 blanc		8 marron	
9 orange		10 gris		11 violet		12 beige	

 **Colorie le dessin.**

Et maintenant

Translation *Colours. Colour each square with the correct colour.* • *Colour the drawing.* **Teachers' note** You could photocopy other black and white line illustrations and number them in the same way. Give them to the children to colour in using the key on this page.

Developing French
Livre Deux
A & C Black

Les vêtements noirs et blancs

✎ **Ecris les couleurs.**

Liste		
blanc	blanches	noirs
blanche	noir	noires
blancs	noire	

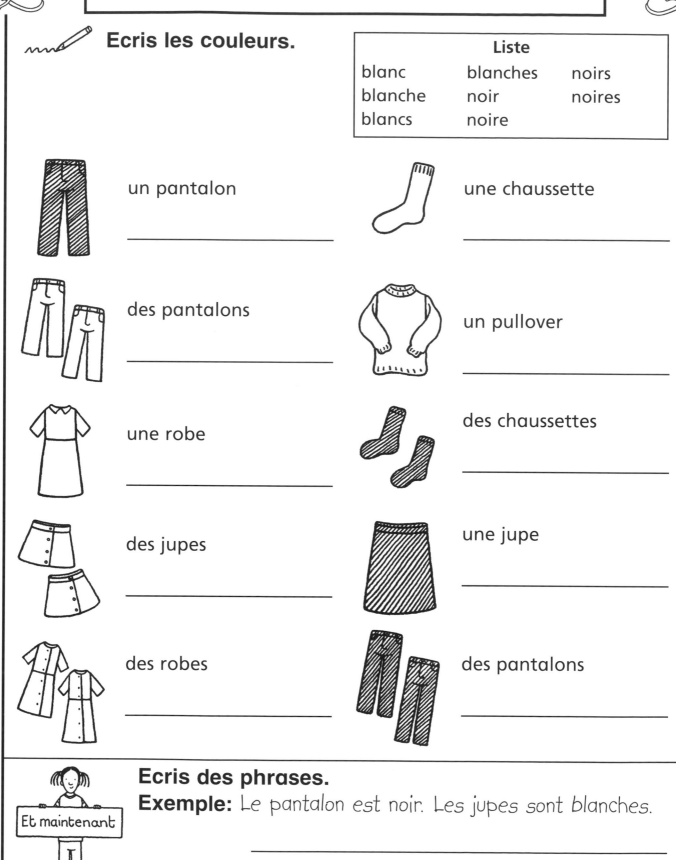

un pantalon

_____

une chaussette

_____

des pantalons

_____

un pullover

_____

une robe

_____

des chaussettes

_____

des jupes

_____

une jupe

_____

des robes

_____

des pantalons

_____

Ecris des phrases.

Exemple: Le pantalon est noir. Les jupes sont blanches.

Et maintenant

_____

_____

_____

Translation *Black and white clothes. Write the colours.* • *Write sentences. Example: The trousers are black. The skirts are white.* **Teachers' note** In this activity, the children have to choose the colour adjective with the correct ending, paying attention to whether the noun is masculine or feminine and singular or plural. For the extension, revise *est* and *sont*, and emphasise the difference between them.

Developing French
Livre Deux
A & C Black

22

Compréhension

 Regarde le texte.

 **Réponds aux questions.**

Colorie l'image.

Jacques et Stéphanie habitent dans une maison. Dans la chambre de Jacques il y a un lit bleu et une table verte. Stéphanie a une table jaune et une lampe rose. Ils ont un chat noir et blanc qui s'appelle Minet et un oiseau vert et jaune qui s'appelle Coco. Dans le salon, le canapé est marron et les fauteuils sont beiges.

   Aujourd'hui Stéphanie porte une robe orange et un collant violet. Jacques porte toujours une casquette rouge.

Dictionnaire

Questions

1. De quelle couleur est le lit de Jacques?_____

2. De quelle couleur est la lampe de Stéphanie?_____

3. Combien d'animaux est-ce qu'ils ont?_____

4. De quelle couleur est le chat?_____

5. Comment s'appelle le chat?_____

6. De quelle couleur est le canapé?_____

7. Où est le canapé?_____

8. De quelle couleur est le collant de Stéphanie?_____

9. De quelle couleur est la casquette de Jacques?_____

10. Qui est Coco?_____

Et maintenant

Dessine Stéphanie et Jacques et les animaux dans la maison.

Translation *Comprehension. Look at the text. Answer the questions. Colour the picture.*
• *Draw Stéphanie and Jacques and the animals in the house.* **Teachers' note** This comprehension text combines a variety of topics. Provide a dictionary so that the children can look up any words they have forgotten.

Developing French
Livre Deux
A & C Black

Les nombres de 40 à 100

 Découpe les cartes.

 Mets les cartes en paires.

quatre-vingt-quatre	soixante-trois	quatre-vingt-un	soixante-dix
quatre-vingt-treize	quatre-vingt-dix-sept	cinquante-deux	quatre-vingt-dix
soixante et onze	quatre-vingt-onze	cent	quatre-vingt-cinq
quatre-vingt-neuf	quarante	quatre-vingt-dix-huit	soixante
quarante et un	soixante-quatorze	quatre-vingts	cinquante

40	50	60	70	41
52	63	71	80	81
84	85	89	90	91
93	98	74	97	100

Translation *Numbers 40 to 100. Cut out the cards. Put the cards in pairs.* **Teachers' note** This activity helps the children to learn numbers up to 100. Once the children have matched the pairs, they could glue the numbers in words on to a large piece of paper, with the matching numbers in figures beneath. Alternatively, they can glue the whole sheet on to card and cut it up to make flashcards. The cards can be used for card games and bingo (see page 19).

Developing French
Livre Deux
A & C Black

C'est combien?

 Regarde les vêtements.

 Regarde les phrases.

Ecris les prix sur les dessins.

- Le pantalon coûte trente-cinq euros.
- La chemise coûte cinquante et un euros.
- La robe coûte quarante-six euros.
- L'anorak coûte soixante-douze euros.
- La jupe coûte trente-huit euros.
- Le pullover coûte soixante-trois euros.

Ecris le prix en lettres.

Le pullover et le pantalon, c'est combien?

_____

La chemise et la jupe, c'est combien?

_____

Translation *How much is it? Look at the clothes. Look at the sentences. Write the prices on the drawings. • Write the price in words.* **Teachers' note** Use this activity to reinforce the vocabulary for clothes and prices (involving numbers up to 100).

Developing French
Livre Deux
A & C Black

Le shopping

 Regarde la liste.

 **Complète les bulles.**

Liste	
Au revoir	C'est combien
Bonjour	Madame
Je voudrais	Au revoir
s'il vous plaît	Merci
couleur	

 Bonjour Madame!

_____ Madame! Vous désirez?

_____ un pantalon, s'il vous plaît.

De quelle _____?

 Bleu, _____.

Voilà, Madame.

Merci Madame. _____?

Trente euros, _____.

 Voilà! _____.

_____ Madame. _____.

 **Pratique la conversation avec ton/ta partenaire.**

Translation *Shopping. Look at the list. Complete the bubbles. • Practise the conversation with your partner.* **Teachers' note** This activity provides an opportunity to practise the vocabulary and dialogue of shopping. For the extension, the children can write their conversation in their notebook or on a separate sheet of paper. They could modify their conversations to include other types of clothing, colours and prices.

Developing French
Livre Deux
A & C Black

Portrait

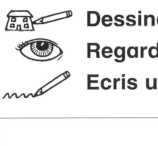 **Dessine-toi en couleurs.**

Regarde la liste.

Ecris une description.

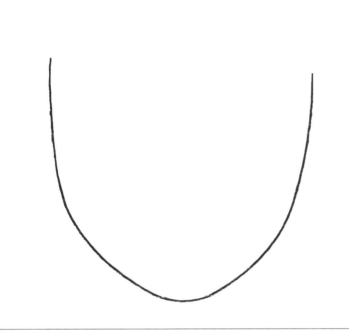

Liste	
j'ai	les cheveux
il a	châtains
elle a	bruns
les yeux	roux
blues	gris
marron	blancs
gris	
verts	

Je m'appelle _____

_____ .

J'ai _____

_____ .

J'ai _____

_____ .

Dessine deux membres de ta famille.

Ecris une description.

Exemple: *C'est ma sœur.*

Elle a les cheveux blonds.

Liste
mon père
ma mère
mon grand-père
ma grand-mère
ma sœur
mon frère

Et maintenant

_____   _____

_____   _____

Translation *Portrait. Draw yourself in colour. Look at the list. Write your description.*
• *Draw two members of your family. Write a description.* **Teachers' note** In this activity, the children practise describing the colour of hair and eyes. Encourage them to check they have used the correct adjective ending by looking at the list. In the extension encourage them to use *il a.../ elle a...*

Developing French
Livre Deux
A & C Black

Picture dictionary

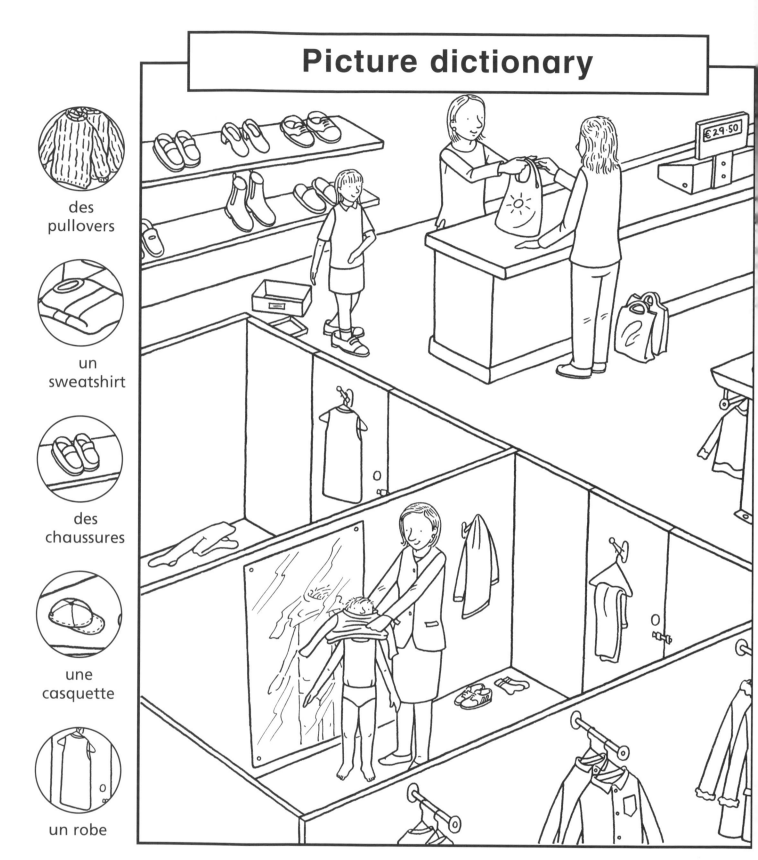

des
pullovers

un
sweatshirt

des
chaussures

une
casquette

un robe

des
chaussettes

un collant

une jupe

un pantalon

une
chemise

un blouson

€29·50

Developing French
Livre Deux
A & C Black

28

Le corps et les vêtements

des parapluies

un sac

un imperméable

une ceinture

des slips

des chemisettes

des bottes

une veste

un short

un chapeau

des T-shirts

Developing French
Livre Deux
A & C Black

Topic 3: La nourriture et la boisson

Key vocabulary and grammar

Vocabulary to be used by the children:

du pain	bread
du beurre	butter
de la confiture	jam
du miel	honey
des céréales	cereal
des œufs (un œuf)	eggs (an egg)
de la viande	meat
du poisson	fish
des pommes de terre	potatoes
des frites	chips
des pâtes	pasta
du riz	rice
des légumes	vegetables
de la glace	ice cream
un gâteau	a cake
de la soupe	soup
un sandwich	a sandwich
du fromage	cheese
des fruits/un fruit	fruit/a piece of fruit
du chocolat	chocolate/hot chocolate
du café	coffee
du thé	tea
du lait	milk
du coca (cola)	cola
du jus d'orange	orange juice
du vin (rouge/blanc)	(red/white) wine
de la limonade	lemonade
de la bière	beer
de l'eau minérale	mineral water
Tu veux du.../	Would you like
de la.../des...	some...?
Oui, j'aime ça	Yes, I like that
Non, je n'aime pas ça	No, I don't like that
J'ai faim	I'm hungry
J'ai soif	I'm thirsty
le petit déjeuner	breakfast
le déjeuner	lunch
le goûter	afternoon snack
le dîner	dinner/evening meal
un verre	a glass
une tasse	a cup
une assiette	a plate
un bol	a bowl
une fourchette	a fork
une cuillère	a spoon
un couteau	a knife
Pour... il faut...	In order to... you need...

Grammar to be used by the children:
• negative verb construction: ne... pas

For recognition only:

Qu'est-ce que	What do you
tu manges/bois?	eat/drink?

Teaching ideas

Introducing food and drink names

Introduce the new vocabulary using flashcards (you could enlarge the ones on page 32). Alternatively, use real food. This is especially appropriate for dry goods (pasta and rice), packets (cereal), tins (vegetables, fish, fruit); plastic replica fruit, vegetables and meat can be bought from toy or educational shops. When teaching the children *un œuf/des œufs*, note that in the singular the *f* is pronounced but in the plural both the *f* and the *s* are silent.

Ask the question *Tu veux... (de la viande/des frites)?* as you hold up the appropriate visual aid. The children should reply either *Oui, j'aime ça* or *Non, je n'aime pas ça*. As they answer, they could make the appropriate face, give thumbs up or thumbs down, or hold up cards showing smiling or grimacing faces.

Asking for food and drink

Once the children have repeated and practised all the food words, invite them to ask you for items of food: for example, *Je voudrais du pain/de la confiture/des frites s'il vous plaît*. If children ask correctly, give them the item of food they asked for.

After this, play a game in which the children ask each other for items of food. Distribute the items among the children and choose one child to begin asking (using *s'il vous plaît* if they are asking the teacher or *s'il te plaît* if asking another pupil). Encourage them to say *merci* when they receive the item. As long as the child does not make a mistake, he or she may carry on asking the others for food. If the child dries up or makes a mistake, the person who was being asked takes over. Whoever has the most at the end of the game wins (the game can end at any time, or when one child has succeeded in collecting all the food). Once the words for drinks have been learnt, these can be used in the game too.

Introduce the phrases *j'ai faim* and *j'ai soif*, either using actions or by telling the children the English translations. Then encourage the children to

combine them with the phrases already learned, for example: *J'ai faim, je voudrais des fruits. J'ai soif, je voudrais du lait.* Point out that when ordering drinks in a café or restaurant, it is necessary to use *un* or *une* instead of *du/de la/de l'*, for example, *Je voudrais un café* instead of *Je voudrais du café*.

Names of meals
Teach the names of the meals by translating them into English or using visual aids such as clocks and pictures. Explain that in France *le goûter* is a necessary snack since the evening meal tends to be eaten much later than in Britain. Then ask the children to say what they have for each meal using the prompts *Qu'est-ce que tu manges au petit déjeuner? Qu'est-ce que tu bois?* The children should begin their answer *Je mange...* or *Je bois...* Visual aids can be held up by both the teacher and the person answering the question. This will help everyone to remember what is being talked about, especially those children needing more support.

Names of crockery and cutlery
Introduce the words for crockery and cutlery by showing the children real items or pictures. Once the children are confident with the vocabulary, they can make up sentences explaining which crockery and cutlery they would use for different foods and drinks, for example, *Pour manger de la soupe, il faut un bol et une cuillère.*

Further activities

Page 32 Practising items of food These cards can be enlarged, glued on to card and used for quick-fire vocabulary practise. Hold up a card and ask *Qu'est-ce que c'est?* Alternatively, let the children make their own sets of flashcards, then ask questions which they can answer by holding up the correct card. They can use the picture and word cards to play matching pairs games, Snap and Pelmanism.

Page 32 Playing *Loto* (bingo) Divide the class into two teams. Cut the pictures on the sheet into two sets to make two *Loto* cards, each with ten pictures (you could glue these on to card or laminate them). Give a *Loto* card and ten counters to each team. Then call out the French names of the items on the cards, one at a time. The players in each team confer and place a counter on the correct picture if they have it. When a team covers all their objects, they should call out *Loto*. Check their card in case they have made a mistake. For additional points they could be asked to say the names of all the items on their card.

Page 37 Practising crockery, cutlery, food and drink When the children have completed the activity and placed the dominoes in a line or circle, ask them to make up sentences using the items on the cards and the verbs *manger* or *boire*, for example, *Pour boire du thé, il faut une tasse.*

La nourriture

 Découpe les cartes.

 Mets les mots avec les dessins.

  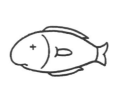  

   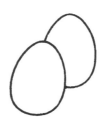 

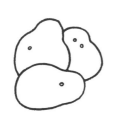    

du poisson	de la soupe	des fruits	des céréales	du beurre
du pain	des légumes	un sandwich	des œufs	des pommes de terre
de la confiture	des frites	des pâtes	un gâteau	du chocolat
une glace	de la viande	du riz	du fromage	du miel

Translation *Food. Cut out the cards. Put the words with the drawings.* **Teachers' note** This activity helps the children to learn the words for items of food. Once the children have matched the pairs, they could glue the pictures and matching captions on to a large piece of paper. Alternatively, glue the whole sheet on to card and cut it up to make flashcards. The cards can be used for card games and bingo (see page 31).

Developing French
Livre Deux
A & C Black

La boisson

 Regarde les dessins.

 Regarde la liste.

 Ecris les mots.

Liste

de la limonade   du vin
du coca   du lait
du thé   du chocolat
du café   de l'eau minérale
du jus d'orange

du thé   _____   _____   _____

_____   _____   _____   _____

Ecris les boissons.

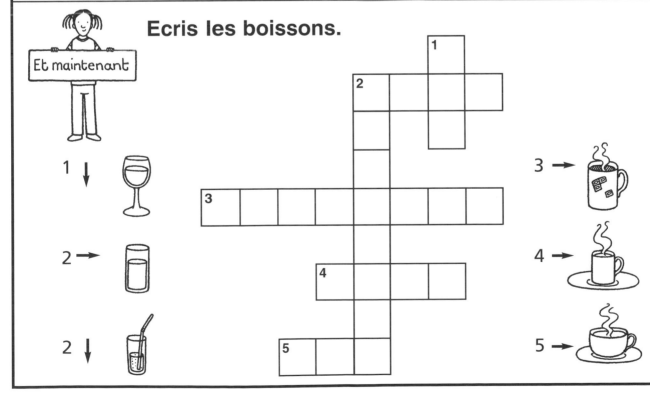

Translation *Drink. Look at the drawings. Look at the list. Write the words. • Write the drinks.*
Teachers' note This activity involves practising the words for drinks. For the extension, explain that the arrows show the direction in which the answers should be written in the grid. Tell the children to write the answers in capital letters (i.e. without accents).

Developing French
Livre Deux
A & C Black

Qu'est-ce que tu aimes?

 Regarde la liste.

 Ecris ce que tu aimes.

Ecris ce que tu n'aimes pas.

Liste
le pain
le beurre
le miel
la confiture
les céréales
les œufs
la viande
le poisson
les pommes de terre
les frites
le riz
les légumes
la glace
les gâteaux
la soupe
les sandwichs
le fromage
les fruits
le chocolat

J'aime…

Je n'aime pas…

_____

_____

_____

_____

_____

_____

_____

Et maintenant

Demande à ton/ta partenaire:

Qu'est-ce que tu aimes?

Qu'est-ce que tu n'aimes pas?

Ecris les réponses.

Mon/ma partenaire s'appelle _____.

Il/Elle aime _____.

Il/Elle n'aime pas_____.

Translation *What do you like?* *Look at the list. Write what you like. Write what you don't like.* • *Ask your partner for their likes and dislikes. Write their answers.* **Teachers' note** In this activity the children practise using the verb *aimer* and the negative construction *ne... pas*. They also revise the names of items of food. In the extension, encourage the children to reply to the questions in sentences, for example. *J'aime le miel. Je n'aime pas le riz.*

Developing French
Livre Deux
A & C Black

J'ai faim, j'ai soif

  Regarde la liste.

Complète les phrases.

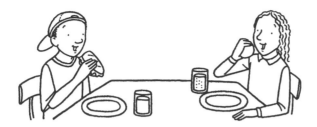

J'ai faim, je voudrais <u>du pain</u> .

J'ai soif, je voudrais de <u>la limonade</u> .

 J'ai faim, je voudrais _____ .

J'ai faim, je voudrais _____ .

 J'ai soif, je _____ .

J'ai _____ , _____ .

J'ai _____ , _____ .

 J'ai _____ , _____ .

 **Regarde la liste.**

Ecris une conversation.

Et maintenant

Liste
s'il vous plaît
s'il te plaît
voilà
merci
du chocolat
j'ai faim
je voudrais

_____

_____

_____

_____

_____

Translation *I am hungry, I am thirsty. Look at the list. Complete the sentences .• Look at the list. Write a conversation.* **Teachers' note** This activity helps the children to express what they would like to eat or drink. Explain that they should complete all the sentences following the same model. In the extension activity, suggest that they begin the conversation with a sentence similar to those in the main activity. They could practise the conversation with a partner.

Developing French
Livre Deux
A & C Black

Au café-restaurant

 Regarde le menu.

 Complète la conversation.

Menu

steak frites	8 €	thé	4 €
hot-dog	5,50 €	café	3 €
sandwichs	4,50 €	coca	2 €
hamburger	6 €	limonade	1,50 €
frites	2 €	jus de fruits	3,50 €

Sophie: Des sandwichs et des frites pour tout le monde?

Marie: Oui. Tu veux un jus de fruits, Sophie?

Sophie: Non, je voudrais _____ _____ .

Pierre: Moi, _____ _____ une limonade, et toi Jamel?

Jamel: Un coca.

Le garçon: Vous avez choisi?

Sophie: Oui, quatre _____ et des _____ s'il vous plaît.

Et un coca, une limonade, un jus de fruits et un café.

Le garçon: Voilà, _____ sandwichs, des frites, un _____ ,

une _____ , un _____ ___ _____ ,

un _____ .

Pierre: Ça fait combien?

Le garçon: 36 euros, s'il vous plaît.

Pierre: Voilà.

Le garçon: Merci, Monsieur.

 **Qu'est-ce que tu choisis? Ça fait combien?**

_____ € _____

Translation *At the café-restaurant. Look at the menu. Complete the conversation.* • *What would you like? How much is it?* **Teachers' note** This conversation deals with how to order food and drinks in a café. Tell the children to read through the entire conversation before beginning, and again at the end to check it makes sense. In the extension, the children should choose food and drink from the menu and work out how much they have to pay.

Developing French
Livre Deux
A & C Black

Avec quoi?

 Regarde les dessins.

 Regarde la liste.

 Ecris les mots.

Liste	
du thé	un couteau
de la soupe	un verre
un bol	une assiette
une tasse	du coca
une cuillère	des frites
des céréales	une fourchette
du fromage	des pâtes

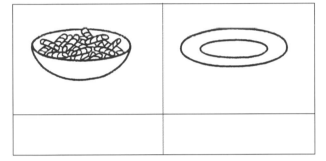

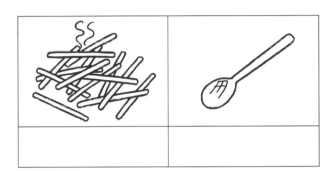

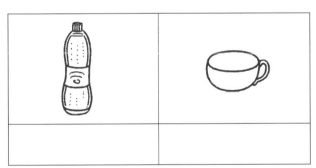

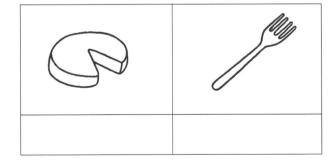

 **Découpe les dominos. Mets-les en paires.**

Et maintenant

Translation *With what? Look at the drawings. Look at the list. Write the words.* • *Cut out the dominoes. Pair them up.* **Teachers' note** This activity combines practising the words for crockery and cutlery with revision of food and drink. When matching up the dominoes, the children should match each food or drink with a piece of crockery or cutlery (there may be more than one possibility). All the dominoes can be joined in a line or circle.

Developing French
Livre Deux
A & C Black

Picture dictionary

du pain

de la
confiture

des
céréales

des œufs

de la
viande

Café

du
poisson

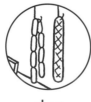

des
saucisses

du
fromage

des
pommes

des poires

du lait

Developing French
Livre Deux
A & C Black

38

Au supermarché

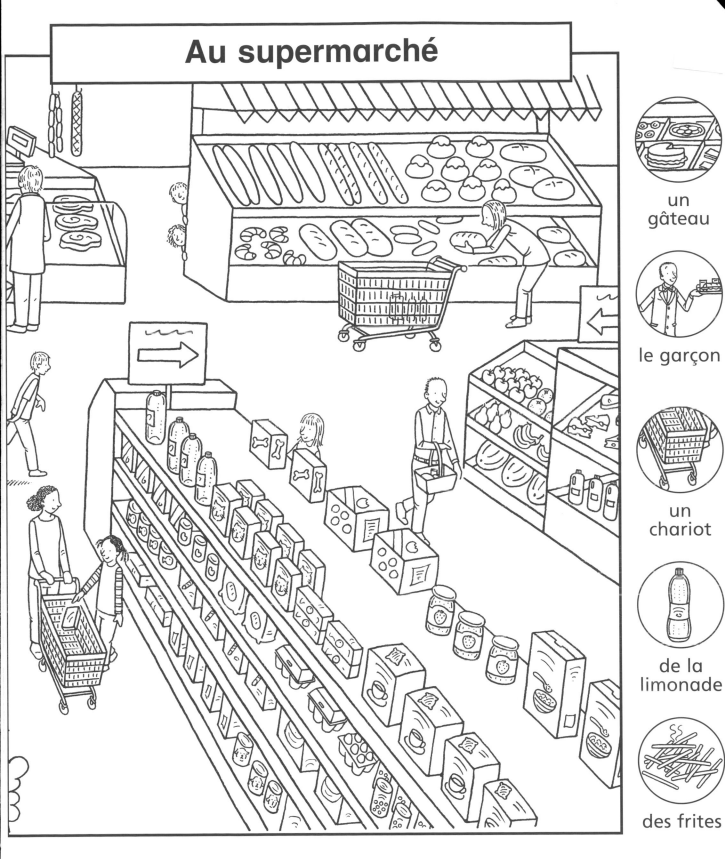

un
gâteau

le garçon

un
chariot

de la
limonade

des frites

du café

du thé

du coca

de la
soupe

du vin

des pâtes

Topic 4: Ma ville

Key vocabulary and grammar

For revision:

Names of items of food and drink

The verb *être* (to be):

je suis	I am
tu es	you are
il/elle est	he/she is
nous sommes	we are
vous êtes	you are
ils/elles sont	they are

Vocabulary to be used by the children:

Où habites-tu?	Where do you live?
j'habite à...	I live in...
près/loin	close/far
ma rue	my street
une ville	a town
un village	a village
une école	a school
une bibliothèque	a library
une église	a church
une gare	a railway station
une poste	a post office
une piscine	a swimming pool
une banque	a bank
un café	a café
un hôtel	a hotel
l'hôtel de ville	the town hall
une boulangerie	a baker's shop
une pâtisserie	a cake shop
une boucherie	a butcher's shop
une charcuterie	a delicatessen
une épicerie	a grocer's shop
une poissonnerie	a fishmonger's shop
une librairie	a bookshop
un marchand	a seller
un marchand de légumes/primeurs	a greengrocer
un (bureau de) tabac	a tobacconist
un supermarché	a supermarket
à côté de	next to
en face de	opposite
entre	between
il y a...	there is/there are
on achète...	you can buy
à la.../au...	at
tournez à gauche	turn left
tournez à droite	turn right
allez tout droit	go straight on
Où est le/la...?	Where is the...?

Pour aller à la.../au...?	Can you tell me the way to the...?
première/deuxième/ troisième (rue) à droite/gauche	first/second/third road on the right/left

numbers 101 to 999 999:
cent un (101), *cent deux* (102), *cent trois* (103), *deux cents* (200), *deux cent un* (201), *deux cent deux* (202), *deux cent trois* (203), *mille* (1000), *onze cent un* (1101), *deux mille trois cent dix* (2310), *deux cent mille* (200 000)...

For recognition only:

du jambon	ham
du pâté	paté
des saucisses	sausages
de l'aspirine	aspirin
des livres	books
des timbres	stamps

Teaching ideas

Saying where you live

Introduce how to say in which town and country you live, for example, *J'habite à Londres, en Angleterre/J'habite à Cardiff, au pays de Galles.* Use *en Angleterre* (in England), *au pays de Galles* (in Wales), *en Ecosse* (in Scotland), *en Irlande du Nord* (in Northern Ireland) or *en Irlande* (in the Irish Republic/Eire), as appropriate. You could use a map of the country as a visual aid. Encourage the children to practise asking and answering the question *Où habites-tu?*

Names of places in the local area

Introduce the names of the main buildings in a town using flashcards made from the activity sheet on page 43. Then display a large photocopy of the town plan on page 46. Write the phrases *c'est près* and *c'est loin* on the board. Point to the child on the plan and then to a building such as the post office as you say: *La poste, c'est près ou c'est loin?* Mime short and long distances as you ask the question, and give the answer yourself until the children are ready to take over. Repeat for all the buildings on the plan.

Understanding and giving simple directions

To introduce giving directions, do actions for *tout droit*, *à droite* and *à gauche*. Make sure you do this while facing the same way as the children, so that they do not confuse right and left. Ask for a volunteer to help you demonstrate *va/allez* and *tourne/tournez*; tell the child to go or turn in a certain direction and make gestures to help him/her understand your instructions. When several children have had a go at following your commands, invite one of the children to give commands to the others. It can be fun to set up a simple obstacle course (using classroom furniture). Blindfold a volunteer and challenge the rest of the class to give directions to guide the blindfolded child around the obstacles.

After this, you can teach the children how to ask for and give directions in a town. Display a large photocopy of the town plan on page 46. Alternatively, you can 'build' a town in the classroom by arranging the tables to make blocks of buildings with 'streets' between, and putting pictures of various buildings on the tables. Ask the question *Où est le/la…?* or *Pour aller à la…/au…?* (followed by the name of a building). Add *s'il vous plaît* in both cases. Phrases which can be used in the answer include *allez tout droit, tournez à droite/gauche* and *première/deuxième/troisième (rue) à droite/gauche*.

Names of shops

Before starting on the names of shops it is advisable to revise food and drink. Add the names of other items sold in the shops: *du jambon, du pâté*, and *des saucisses* in the *charcuterie*; *de l'aspirine* in the *pharmacie*; *des livres* in the *librairie*; and *des timbres* in the *tabac*.

Display an enlarged photocopy of the activity sheet on page 44 with the names of the shops written in. Introduce the names of the shops and let the children practise repeating them. At this point it is helpful to explain briefly (in English) about French shopping habits, for example buying bread daily from *une boulangerie*. Link the names of the shops with the items that can be bought in them, for example: *Pour acheter du pain, on va à la boulangerie* or *À la boulangerie, on achète du pain*. Again using the illustration from page 44, ask the children to imagine that the rows of shops represent streets in a town. Introduce *entre, à côté de* and *en face de* using the question *Où est…?* (followed by the name of a shop).

Numbers beyond 100

First revise numbers up to 100 (see explain that for numbers beyond simply add *cent, deux cents, trois* [but no *s* on *cent* if followed by t the beginning, for example, *cent cent trois… deux cent un, deux c cent trois.* Then introduce the word *mille*. Explain that they have now learnt all the vocabulary they need in order to be able to count up to 999 999!

Further activities

Pages 43 and 44 Practising names of buildings and shops These cards can be enlarged, glued on to card and used for quick-fire vocabulary practice. Hold up a card and ask *Qu'est-ce que c'est?* Alternatively, let the children make their own sets of cards, then ask questions which they can answer by holding up the correct card. The children could make extra sets of cards showing the French words for the buildings or shops pictured on the cards. They can then use these with the unlabelled picture cards to play matching pairs games, Snap and Pelmanism.

Page 43 Playing *Loto* (bingo) Divide the class into two teams. Cut the pictures on the sheet into two sets to make two *Loto* cards, each with five pictures (you could glue these on to card or laminate them). Give a *Loto* card and five counters to each team. Then call out the French names of the buildings on the cards, one at a time. The players in each team confer and place a counter on the correct picture if they have it. When a team covers all their buildings, they should call out *Loto*. Check their card in case they have made a mistake. For additional points they could be asked to say the names of all the buildings on their card.

Page 44 Playing *Loto* (bingo) The pictures on this page can be combined with those on page 43 to make a more challenging game of *Loto*. Cut the pictures on this sheet into two sets to make two more *Loto* cards, each with four pictures. Give each team one card from this page and one card from page 43, and nine counters. Then play *Loto* as described above. The children have to cover all the pictures on both their cards before calling out *Loto*.

Page 49 Revising buildings and shops Once the children have finished the activity, you could ask them to colour the pictures according to whether the noun is masculine or feminine (using two different colours).

J'habite à . . .

👁 **Regarde la carte.**

✏ **Complète les phrases.**

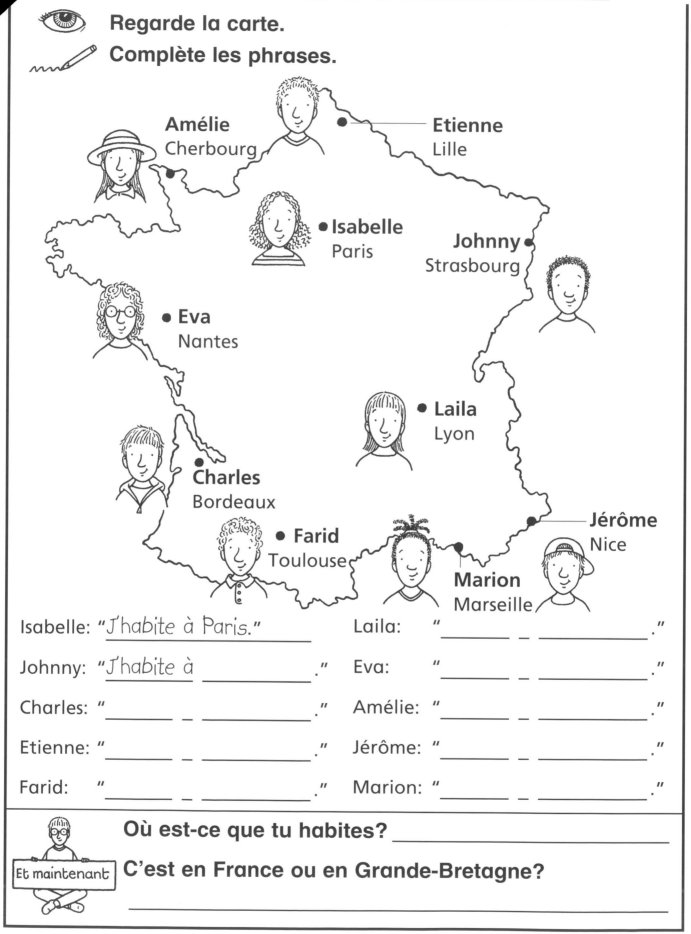

Amélie
Cherbourg

Etienne
Lille

Isabelle
Paris

Johnny
Strasbourg

Eva
Nantes

Laila
Lyon

Charles
Bordeaux

Farid
Toulouse

Marion
Marseille

Jérôme
Nice

Isabelle: "J'habite à Paris."   Laila: "_____ _ _____."

Johnny: "J'habite à _____."   Eva: "_____ _ _____."

Charles: "_____ _ _____."   Amélie: "_____ _ _____."

Etienne: "_____ _ _____."   Jérôme: "_____ _ _____."

Farid: "_____ _ _____."   Marion: "_____ _ _____."

Où est-ce que tu habites? _____

Et maintenant   **C'est en France ou en Grande-Bretagne?**

_____

Translation *I live in... Look at the map. Complete the sentences.* • *Where do you live? Is it in France or in Britain?* **Teachers' note** This activity helps the children to understand the use of *j'habite à* or *en*. It also shows them the shape of France and the location of some major towns and cities. Encourage the children, in pairs, to ask each other where they live. They should give both the town and country in their reply.

Developing French
Livre Deux
A & C Black

Ma ville

 Regarde la liste.

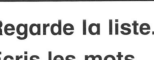 **Ecris les mots.**

Liste
l'hôtel de ville
la gare
l'école
le café
la piscine
la bibliothèque
l'église
l'hôtel
la poste
la banque

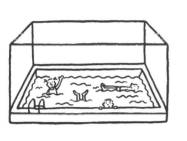

_____

_____

_____

_____

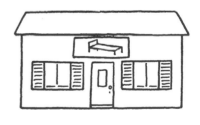

_____

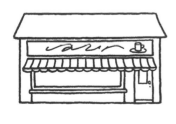

_____

_____

_____

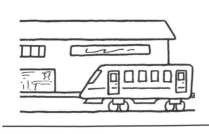

_____

Translation *My town. Look at the list. Write the words.* **Teachers' note** Use this activity to practise the names of buildings. Point out that the clues on the pictures are sometimes given as symbols and ensure that the children recognise the euro sign. Once they have written in the names, they can glue the sheet on to card and cut it up to make flashcards. Alternatively, they can use the unlabelled pictures for card games and bingo (see page 41).

Developing French
Livre Deux
A & C Black

Les magasins

 Regarde la liste.

Ecris les noms des magasins.

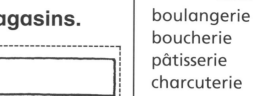

boulangerie

Démêle les mots.

Et maintenant

campahire _____   bariloungee _____

corehubie _____   carumspheré _____

Translation *Shops. Look at the list. Write the names of the shops. • Unjumble the words.*
Teachers' note Use this activity to practise the names of shops. Encourage the children to look
carefully at the illustrations to see what each shop is selling. Once they have written the names,
they can glue the sheet on to card and cut it up to make flashcards. Alternatively, they can use
the unlabelled pictures for card games and bingo (see page 41).

Developing French
Livre Deux
A & C Black

Où est...?

👁 **Regarde le dessin.**

👁 **Regarde les phrases.**

✎ **Marque vrai ou faux.**

	vrai	faux
1. L'église est entre l'épicerie et la boucherie.	✔	
2. L'école est à côté de la poste.		
3. La pharmacie est en face de la gare.		
4. Le café est entre l'hôtel de ville et la librairie.		
5. L'hôtel est à côté de la gare.		
6. L'épicerie est en face de la pâtisserie.		
7. La gare est entre la poste et l'hôtel.		
8. L'école est en face de l'hôtel.		
9. La charcuterie est à côté du café.		

Ecris encore des phrases.

Et maintenant

_____

_____

_____

_____

Translation *Where is...?* Look at the drawing. Look at the sentences. Mark true or false. • Write *some more sentences.* **Teachers' note** This activity involves revising the names of shops and buildings, and using phrases which describe position: *entre, à côté de* and *en face de*. Use this when the children are familiar with the way the shops and buildings are represented on pages 43 and 44.

Developing French
Livre Deux
A & C Black

Pour aller à...

 Regarde le dessin.

 Regarde la liste.

 Réponds aux questions.

Liste	
première	à droite
deuxième	allez tout droit
troisième	le café
à gauche	la librairie

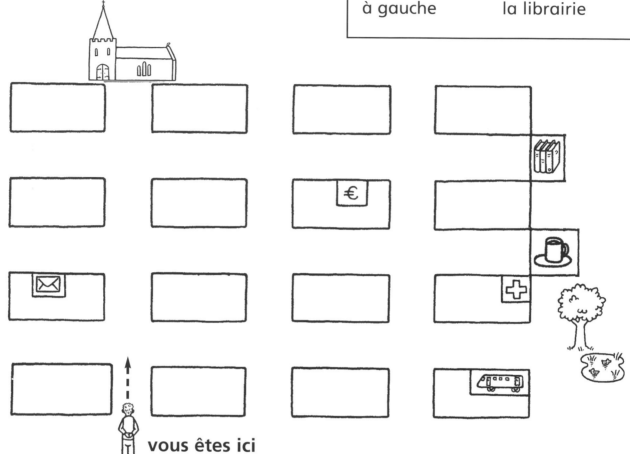

vous êtes ici

Pour aller à la pharmacie, s'il vous plaît? _deuxième à droite_

Pour aller à la gare, s'il vous plaît?_____

Pour aller à l'église, s'il vous plaît?_____

Pour aller à la poste, s'il vous plaît?_____

Pour aller à la banque, s'il vous plaît?_____

 **Où est...**

première à droite, deuxième à gauche et deuxième à droite?_____

deuxième à droite et allez tout droit?_____

Translation *What is the way to...? Look at the drawings. Look at the list. Answer the questions.*
• *Where is...* **Teachers' note** This activity provides practice in giving directions. Ensure the children can identify the buildings correctly from the symbols. The names of all the buildings appear either in the list or in the questions.

Developing French
Livre Deux
A & C Black

Où est-ce qu'on achète ça?

 Relie les mots aux magasins.

- des saucisses ●
- ● du bacon ●
- ● du fromage ●
- ● du riz ●
- ● un éclair ●
- ● des gâteaux ●

- ● des pâtes ●
- ● de l'aspirine ●
- ● un stylo ●
- ● de la viande ●
- ● des croissants ●

- ● du poisson ●
- ● un steak ●

- ● du pain ●
- ● un crabe ●
- ● un livre ●

 **Ecris des phrases.**

Et maintenant

Dictionnaire

Exemples: On achète du riz à l'épicerie.

On achète du pain à la boulangerie.

_____

_____

Translation *Where can you buy this? Join the words to the shops. • Write some sentences. Examples: You can buy rice at the grocer's. You can buy bread at the butcher's.*
Teachers' note This activity combines revision of the names of shops with items of food. The children need to decide which shop is most likely to sell each item.

Developing French
Livre Deux
A & C Black

47

On compte jusqu'à 999 999

 Regarde la liste.

 Ecris les nombres en lettres.

	Liste
	1 un
	2 deux
	3 trois
	4 quatre
	5 cinq
	6 six
	7 sept
	8 huit
	9 neuf
	16 seize
	40 quarante
	50 cinquante
	60 soixante
	70 soixante-dix
	71 soixante et onze
	80 quatre-vingts
	81 quatre-vingt-un
	90 quatre-vingt-dix
	91 quatre-vingt-onze
	100 cent
	101 cent un
	202 deux cent deux
	1000 mille

115 _cent quinze_

321 _trois cent vingt et un_

436 _quatre cent trente-six_

159 _____

642 _____

886 _____

973 _____

1325 _mille trois cent vingt-cinq_

3612 _trois mille six cent douze_

7918 _____

9546 _____

6891 _____

16 263 _____

_____

999 999 _____

_____

 **C'est combien?**

Ecris les prix en chiffres.

Deux cent cinquante
mille euros

Treize mille euros

Teachers' notes *Counting up to 999 999. Look at the list. Write the numbers in words.*
• *How much is it? Write the prices in figures.* **Teachers' note** This activity involves revising
numbers up to 100 and practising a range of numbers less than a million. If the children find
the large numbers difficult, encourage them to write them in words in English first, which will
help them to see how many tens, hundreds and thousands there are.

Developing French
Livre Deux
A & C Black

Mots croisés

Regarde les dessins.

Ecris les mots.

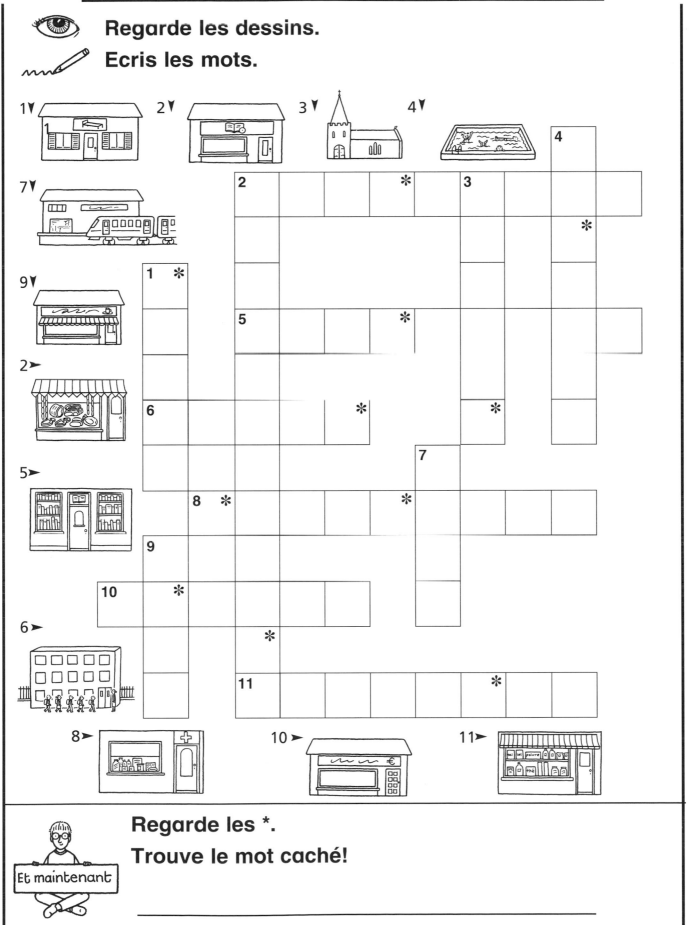

Regarde les *.

Trouve le mot caché!

Translation *Crossword. Look at the drawings. Write the words. • Look at the * . Find the hidden word!* **Teachers' note** Use this activity to revise the vocabulary for shops and buildings. Some children may need the word banks from pages 43 and 44. Tell the children to write the answers in capital letters (i.e. without accents). For the extension, ask them to write down the letters and rearrange them to find the hidden word.

Developing French
Livre Deux
A & C Black

Topic 5: Les transports

Key vocabulary and grammar

For revision:

à (+ name of town)	at/in/to

Vocabulary to be used by the children:

une voiture/une auto	a car
un autobus	a bus
un autocar	a coach
un bateau	a boat
un avion	an aeroplane
un train	a train
une moto	a motorbike
un vélo	a bicycle
en voiture/en auto	by car
en autobus	by bus
en autocar	by coach
en bateau	by boat
en avion/par avion	by aeroplane
par le train	by train
à moto	by motorbike
à vélo	by bicycle
à pied	on foot
en Angleterre	to/in England
en Ecosse	to/in Scotland
au pays de Galles	to/in Wales
en Irlande	to/in Ireland
en France	to/in France

Grammar to be used by the children:

• the verb *aller* (to go):

je vais	I am going/I go
tu vas	you go
il/elle va	he/she goes
(nous allons)	(we go)
(vous allez)	(you go) (polite/plural)
ils/elles vont	they go

• the verb *venir* (to come):

je viens	I am coming/I come
tu viens	you come
il/elle vient	he/she comes
(nous venons)	(we come)
(vous venez)	(you come) (polite/plural)
ils/elles viennent	they come

For recognition only:

Où vas-tu?	Where are you going?
Comment?	How?

Names of countries, for example:

en Belgique	to/in Belgium
en Italie	to/in Italy
en Espagne	to/in Spain
en Suisse	to/in Switzerland
aux Pays-Bas	to/in the Netherlands
en Allemagne	to/in Germany
aux Etats-Unis	to/in the United States
en Afrique	to/in Africa
en Russie	to/in Russia
au Japon	to/in Japan
en Australie	to/in Australia
au Brésil	to/in Brazil
en Inde	to/in India

Teaching ideas

Names of means of transport
Enlarge the pictures on page 52 and cut them out to make flashcards. Use them to introduce the names for the various means of transport. Alternatively, use toys or model vehicles if any are readily available. Discuss briefly the route of the Eurostar and explain that French intercity trains are often referred to as TGV (*trains à grande vitesse* – high speed trains).

The verb *aller*
Teach the verb *aller* by walking round the classroom alone or in groups to illustrate the various pronouns: for example, walk on your own to demonstrate *je vais*. Then ask one child or more to walk with you to demonstrate *nous allons*. Ask a child to walk on his or her own and address the child with *tu vas*. Continue in a similar way for the other forms of the verb. To use the verb *aller* in sentences, walk to the door or window as you say *je vais à la porte/à la fenêtre*. (Only use this for the door and the window, since for some other objects it is is advisable to use *jusqu'à* instead of *à*).

Saying where you are going

Display a large map of France (you could mask out the children's names and faces on page 42 and use an enlarged version of this map). Point to towns or cities on the map and encourage the children to say *je vais à* (followed by the name of the town). If possible, make a map large enough to lay out on the floor allowing children to walk across it from one place to another (you could draw the map in chalk on the floor). Let children choose which place they want to go to and ask either the child doing the moving or another child to describe the movement using the correct form of the verb *aller*.

Combine this with means of transport by asking the children *Où vas-tu?* They should respond by naming a town or city, for example *à Paris* or *à Marseille*. Follow up their answer by asking *Comment? en voiture? en avion? par le train?* (showing them visual aids for the means of transport as you do so). Once the children can pick a suitable means of transport from the choices you offer, encourage the more confident ones to answer without being prompted. Continue until the whole group can respond without being prompted.

Eventually the children should be able to choose a starting point and destination and say: *Je suis à (Marseille). Je vais à (Lyon) (par le train)*. Make sure the means of transport chosen is a sensible one for the journey being made.

The verb *venir*

Venir can be introduced next, with the same method as for *aller* being used to help the children conjugate it. Emphasise the difference in meaning between the two verbs with hand movements away from the chest for *aller* and towards it for *venir*.

Once the children know the verb *venir*, use it in questions to ask how they come to school: *Comment est-ce que tu viens à l'école?* Start the ball rolling by giving prompts, for example, *Moi, je viens à l'école en voiture, et toi? Tu viens à pied? à vélo?* Continue until the children are able to answer without being prompted.

Further activities

Page 52 Practising names of means of transport
The picture cards can be enlarged, glued on to card and used for quick-fire vocabulary practice. Hold up a card and ask *Qu'est-ce que c'est?* Alternatively, let the children make their own flashcards by gluing the pictures on to card, then ask questions which they can answer by holding up the correct card. They can use the picture and word cards to play matching pairs games, Snap and Pelmanism.

Page 56 Practising the verb *aller* Enlarge the map of the world so that it is large enough to lay out on a table allowing children to finger-walk across it from one place to another. Or use toy people to move on the map. Let children choose a starting city and the city they want to go to. Ask *Où vas-tu...?* (followed by the child's name). The child should reply *Je vais à (Madrid)*. Then ask another child *Où va-t-il/elle?* for the child to reply *Il/elle va à (Madrid)*. Then invite pairs of children to move across the map so that the class can practise using *nous, vous* and *ils/elles*, as appropriate. The children can also be encourage to respond to the question *Comment?* They should give a sensible means of transport for the journey they are making.

Les transports

 Découpe les images.

 Découpe les mots.

 Mets les mots avec les dessins.

un train	un avion	une moto	une voiture
un bateau	un autocar	un vélo	un autobus

Réponds aux questions.

Exemple: Le TGV, qu'est-ce c'est? <u>un train</u>

Une Renault, qu'est-ce c'est? _____

Concorde, qu'est-ce c'est? _____

Eurostar, qu'est-ce c'est? _____

Un taxi, qu'est-ce c'est? _____

Pour le Tour de France, il faut _____

Le Titanic, qu'est-ce c'est? _____

Translation *Transport. Cut out the pictures. Cut out the words. Put the words with the drawings. • Answer the questions.* **Teachers' note** This activity introduces the children to the words for means of transport. Once they have matched the pairs, they could glue the pictures and matching captions on to a large piece of paper. The cards can also be used for card games (see page 51). In the extension, the children should give short answers as shown in the example.

**Developing French
Livre Deux
A & C Black**

Aller

Regarde le verbe __aller__.

Complète les phrases.

Pierre

> Je vais
> à Paris.

Jamel et Marie

> Nous allons
> à New York.

aller
(je) vais
(tu) vas
(il) va
(elle) va
(nous) allons
(vous) allez
(ils) vont
(elles) vont

Il _____ à Paris.

Où _____ -tu, Pierre?

Je _____ à Paris.

Ils _____ à New York.

Où _____ -vous, Jamel et Marie?

Nous _____ à New York.

Fatima

> Je _____
> à Rome.

Sophie et Sonia

> Nous _____
> à Sydney.

Elle _____ à Rome.

Où _____ -tu, Fatima?

Je _____ à Rome.

Elles _____ à Sydney.

Où _____ -vous, Sophie et Sonia?

Nous _____ à Sydney.

Et maintenant

Regarde le verbe __aller__. Choisis les mots.

Complète les phrases.

_____ vais à Londres.   _____ allez à Berlin.

_____ vont à Marseille.   _____ va à Glasgow.

Translation **To go.** Look at the verb 'to go'. Complete the sentences. • Look at the verb 'to go'.
Choose the words. Complete the sentences. **Teachers' note** This activity provides practice in all
the forms of the verb aller. As a further extension, give the children these sentences: 'Thierry is
going to Calais.' 'Sébastien and Nathalie are going to Boulogne.' Ask them to draw the people
and write sentences modelled on those in the main activity.

Developing French
Livre Deux
A & C Black

Voyager

 **Regarde la liste.**

 **Ecris le moyen de transport.**

Liste
en voiture
en autobus
en autocar
en bateau
en avion/par avion
par le train
à moto
à vélo
à pied

Je vais à Paris _____

Tu vas à Londres _____

Il va à Nice _____

Elle va à la bibliothèque _____

Nous allons à la piscine _____

Vous allez à Birmingham _____

Ils vont à l'école _____

Je vais à Calais _____

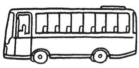

Complète les phrases.

Et maintenant

Tu vas à New York _____

Il va à Liverpool _____

Ecris encore des phrases.

Translation *Travelling. Look at the list. Write the means of transport. • Complete the sentences. Write more sentences.* **Teachers' note** This activity provides practice in using the verb *aller* and describing means of transport. In the extension, make sure the means of transport chosen is suitable for the destination.

Developing French
Livre Deux
A & C Black

Comment tu viens à l'école?

 Regarde les dessins.

 Regarde la liste.

 Complète les phrases.

Liste	
à pied	en autocar
en autobus	en voiture
à vélo	par le train

Sonia — Pierre — Fatima — Jamel — Marie — Thierry

Sonia vient à l'école _____ .

Pierre vient à l'école _____ .

Fatima _____ à l'école _____ .

Jamel _____ l'école _____ .

Marie _____ .

Thierry _____ .

Regarde le verbe <u>venir</u>.

Complète les phrases.

Et maintenant

venir	
(je) viens	(nous) venons
(tu) viens	(vous) venez
(il) vient	(ils) viennent
(elle) vient	(elles) viennent

Nous _____ à l'école à vélo.   Je _____ à l'école à pied.

Ils _____ à l'école par le train.   Il _____ à l'école en voiture.

Elle _____ à l'école à pied.   Elles _____ à l'école à pied.

Tu _____ à l'école à vélo.   Vous _____ à l'école en autobus.

Translation *How do you come to school? Look at the drawings. Look at the list. Complete the sentences. • Look at the verb 'to come'. Complete the sentences.* **Teachers' note** This activity provides practice in the various forms of the verb *venir*, as well as revision of means of transport. As a further extension, ask the children to translate the sentences into English.

Developing French
Livre Deux
A & C Black

C'est loin?

 Regarde la carte.

 Regarde les phrases.

 Marque vrai ou faux.

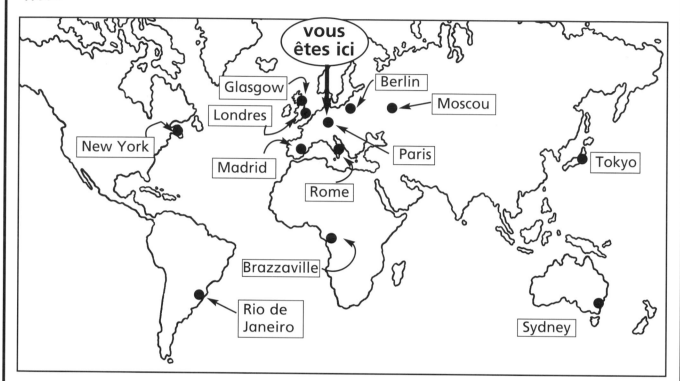

Je suis à Paris.	vrai	faux
Je vais à Rio de Janeiro à pied.		✔
Je vais à Sydney en avion.		
Je vais à Londres en bateau et en voiture.		
Je vais à Moscou par le train.		
Je vais à New York en bateau.		
Je vais à Tokyo à vélo.		
Je vais à Madrid à moto.		

Ecris encore des phrases sur le même modèle.

Et maintenant _____

_____

_____

Translation *Is it far? Look at the map. Look at the sentences. Mark true or false.* • *Write more sentences in the same style.* **Teachers' note** This activity involves revising means of transport and the verb *aller*. Explain that for a sentence to be 'true' it must be reasonably possible. For the extension, ask the children to write 'true' (reasonably possible) sentences

Developing French
Livre Deux
A & C Black

Les drapeaux

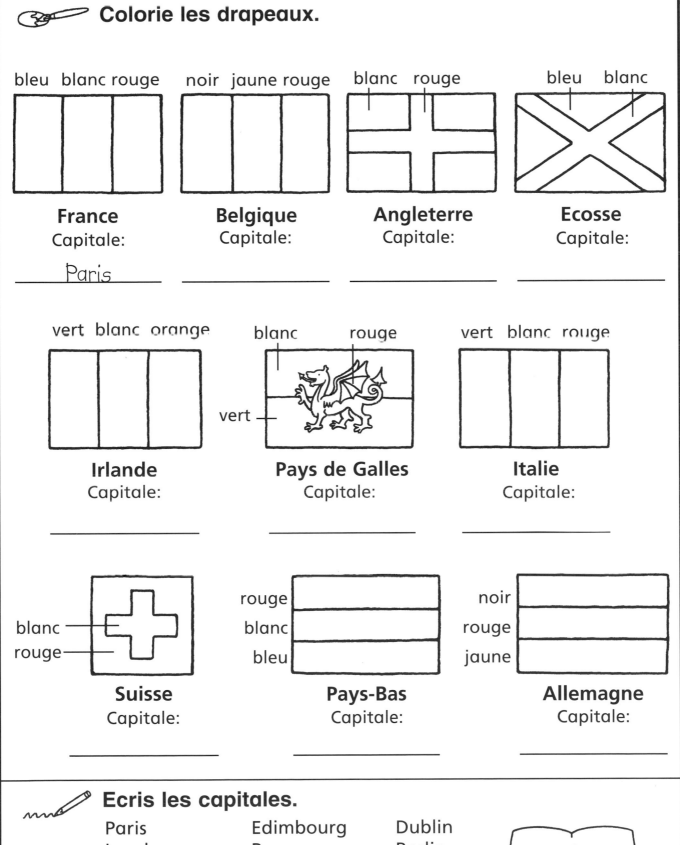

Colorie les drapeaux.

| bleu | blanc | rouge | noir | jaune | rouge | blanc | rouge | bleu | blanc |

France
Capitale:

Paris

Belgique
Capitale:

Angleterre
Capitale:

Ecosse
Capitale:

vert   blanc   orange

blanc   rouge

vert

vert   blanc   rouge

Irlande
Capitale:

Pays de Galles
Capitale:

Italie
Capitale:

blanc
rouge

rouge
blanc
bleu

noir
rouge
jaune

Suisse
Capitale:

Pays-Bas
Capitale:

Allemagne
Capitale:

Ecris les capitales.

Paris	Edimbourg	Dublin
Londres	Rome	Berlin
Cardiff	Berne	
Bruxelles	Amsterdam	

Atlas

Translation *Flags. Colour in the flags. Write the capital cities.* Teachers' note This activity involves learning the words for countries and capital cities, as well as revising colours. Before beginning, check that the children recognise the words for colours.

Developing French
Livre Deux
A & C Black

Le monde

Regarde la liste. **Regarde un atlas.** **Ecris les noms sur la carte.**

Liste
Etats-Unis
Afrique
Ecosse
Pays de Galles
Irlande
Angleterre
France
Russie
Japon
Australie
Brésil
Inde

Atlas

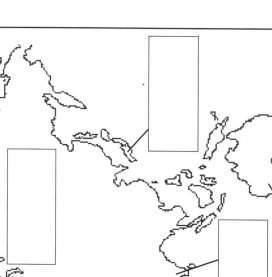

Tu es en Angleterre.
Comment voyages-tu?

Je vais en France _____

Je vais au Japon _____

Je vais au pays de Galles _____

Je vais en Russie _____

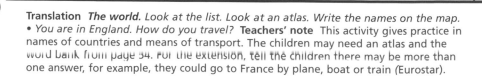
Et maintenant

Je vais en Ecosse _par le train._ _____

Je vais aux Etats-Unis _____

Translation *The world. Look at the list. Look at an atlas. Write the names on the map.*
• *You are in England. How do you travel?* **Teachers' note** This activity gives practice in names of countries and means of transport. The children may need an atlas and the word bank from page 54. For the extension, tell the children there may be more than one answer, for example, they could go to France by plane, boat or train (Eurostar).

Developing French
Livre Deux
A & C Black

La journée de Sophie Durant

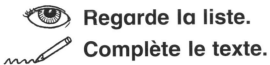 **Regarde la liste.**

Complète le texte.

Liste		
boulangerie	gâteau	pharmacie
casquette	je voudrais	tête
cheveux	mère	train
coca	neuf	verte
fille	noires	viande
frites	père	yeux
gare	pullover	

Sophie Durant est une petite _____ qui a _____ ans.

Elle a les _____ blonds et les _____ bleus. Aujourd'hui

elle porte une jupe _____ , un _____ blanc et des

chaussures _____ . Elle a une _____ noire sur

la _____ .

Elle va au restaurant avec son _____ et sa _____ .

Son père lui demande: "Tu veux un _____ ?"

"Non, _____ une limonade," répond Sophie. Elle mange

de la _____ et des _____ puis un _____

au chocolat.

Après elle fait du shopping. Elle va à la _____ pour

acheter du pain et à la _____ pour acheter de l'aspirine.

Ensuite Monsieur et Madame Durant vont à la _____

prendre le _____ pour rentrer à la maison.

Regarde le texte.

Dessine et colorie Sophie Durant.

Et maintenant

Translation *Sophie Durant's day. Look at the list. Complete the text. • Look at the text. Draw and colour in Sophie.* **Teachers' note** This text includes vocabulary from a range of different topics. Encourage the children to read through the entire text before beginning, and again at the end to check it makes sense. Provide a dictionary so that the children can look up any words they have forgotten.

Developing French
Livre Deux
A & C Black

Picture dictionary

un camion

une bibliothèque

une église

une gare

une poste

une école

une piscine

une banque

un café

un hôtel

une librairie

Developing French
Livre Deux
A & C Black

Dans ma ville

un supermarché

un avion

un bateau

un vélo

une moto

une pharmacie

une voiture

un autobus

un autocar

l'hôtel de ville

un train

Recommended resources

Teaching materials

Pilote by Kent Educational Television, 1992–1993 and and *Pilote plus!* and *Pilote Moi Interactive* by G. Rumley and K. Sharpe, Kent County Council, 2000 and 2002. Videos, teachers' materials, CD-ROMs and resources for use by non-specialist teachers.

Collins Primary French Starter Pack by Helen Morrison, Collins Educational, 2001. Resource pack of books, posters and audio CDs for non-specialist teachers.

EuroTalk Interactive Learn French from Eurotalk Interactive, 315–317 New Kings Road, London SW6 4RF. CD for PC or Macintosh. An audio CD ideal for beginners.

Workbooks

Mon Album á Moi by Danièle Bourdais and Sue Finney, published by Channel 4 Learning, 2001. Activity book.

Jouons avec Gaston by M. Apicella and H. Challier, published by European Language Institute, 1997. Workbooks with puzzles, games and craft activities.

Speak French and *Speak More French* by Opal Dunn, published by Dorling Kindersley, 1995 and 1997. Packs containing workbooks, activity books, board games and cassettes.

Internet linked French for Beginners by Angela Wilkes, published by Usborne, 2001. Book, audio CD, picture dictionary and puzzle-workbook.

Young Explorers: In France by Jane Ellis, published by Egmont World Limited, 2000. Sticker and activity book.

Dictionaries

First Hundred Words in French by Heather Amery and others, published by Usborne, 1988.

First Thousand Words in French by Heather Amery and others, published by Usborne, 1988.

Larousse MINI Débutants published by Larousse in France, 1985–1986.

Websites

www.bbc.co.uk/education/languages/french

Hear French spoken and test your French using simple games, vocabulary and grammar exercises. There is a specific family section.

www.bonjour.org.uk
French-language puzzles and games.

www.kidscrafty.com
French-language puzzles and games specifically for children, but uses US-English translations.

www.ambafrance-uk.org
French Embassy site with details of French education, culture and information about the country. Links to many other French sites in English and French.

Curriculum information and teaching methods

Modern Foreign Languages: A scheme of work for Key Stage 2 published by Qualifications and Curriculum Authority (QCA) 2000, website: www.nc.uk.net

The Centre for Information on Language Teaching and Research (CILT) has an extensive library of books, audio, video and computer software for teaching French (and other modern foreign languages) at all levels. It produces various information sheets and publications and is the National Advisory Centre on Early Language Learning (NACELL).

Contact or visit CILT at 20 Bedfordbury, London WC2 4LB, tel: 020 7379 5110, e-mail: library@cilt.org.uk, website: www.cilt.org.uk

Suppliers of books and teaching materials

Merryman Primary Resources Ltd, PO Box 6718, Bingham, Nottingham, NG13 8QT.
tel: 01949 875 929, e-mail: info@merryman.co.uk, website: www.merryman.co.uk

Bilingual Supplies for Children, PO Box 4081, Bournemouth, Dorset, BH8 9ZZ.
website: www.bilingual-supplies.co.uk

Ecole Alouette, Monkton Road Farm, Birchington, Kent CT7 0JL. tel: 01843 843 447.
e-mail: info@skoldo.com

Early Start Languages, 74 Middle Deal Road, Kent CT14 9RH. tel: 01304 362 569.
e-mail: orders@earlystart.co.uk
website: www.earlystart.co.uk

European Schoolbooks Limited, The Runnings, Cheltenham, Gloucestershire, GL51 9PQ.
tel: 01242 245 252. e-mail: direct@esb.co.uk
websites: www.eurobooks.co.uk

Answers

p 11
Et maintenant

une jambe	*les jambes*
une épaule	*les épaules*
une main	*les mains*
un bras	*les bras*
une oreille	*les oreilles*
un genou	*les genoux*
un pied	*les pieds*

p 13
J'ai mal au pied
J'ai mal au genou
J'ai mal aux yeux
J'ai mal à la tête
J'ai mal à l'oreille
J'ai mal au bras

Illustrations should show:
someone whose leg hurts
someone whose nose hurts

p 14
bouche
jambe
main
genou
oreille
épaules
pied
œil

Et maintenant
nez, corps

p 16
1. *Nous **avons** deux pieds.*
2. *J'**ai** deux épaules.*
3. *Nous **avons** une tête.*
4. *Ils **ont** deux bras.*
5. *Il **a** deux yeux.*
6. *Tu **as** une bouche.*
7. *Elles **ont** un nez.*
8. *Vous **avez** deux oreilles.*
9. *Elle **a** deux mains.*

Et maintenant
1. *oreille*
2. *yeux*
3. *main*
4. *nez*
5. *épaules*
6. *tête*
7. *pied*
8. *bouche*

p 21
Squares and picture should be coloured as follows:
1. red
2. blue
3. yellow
4. green
5. pink
6. black
7. white
8. brown
9. orange
10. grey
11. purple
12. beige

p 22
un pantalon noir	*une chaussette blanche*
des pantalons blancs	*un pullover blanc*
une robe blanche	*des chaussettes noires*
des jupes blanches	*une jupe noire*
des robes blanches	*des pantalons noirs*

Possible sentences are:
Le pantalon est noir.
La chaussette est blanche.
Les pantalons sont blancs.
Le pullover est blanc.
La robe est blanche.
Les chaussettes sont noires.
Les jupes sont blanches.
La jupe est noire.
Les robes sont blanches.
Les pantalons sont noirs.

p 23
1. *(Il est) bleu*
2. *(Elle est) rose*
3. *deux*
4. *(Il est) noir et blanc*
5. *(Il s'appelle) Minet*
6. *(Il est) marron*
7. *(Il est) dans le salon*
8. *(Il est) violet*
9. *(Elle est) rouge*
10. *un oiseau/l'oiseau de Jacques et Stéphanie*

p 25
trousers	*35 euros*
shirt	*51 euros*
dress	*46 euros*
anorak	*72 euros*
skirt	*38 euros*
pullover	*63 euros*

Et maintenant
quatre-vingt-dix-huit euros
quatre-vingt-neuf euros

p 26
Bonjour Madame!
Bonjour Madame! Vous désirez?
Je voudrais un pantalon, s'il vous plaît.
De quelle couleur?
Bleu, s'il vous plaît.
Voilà, Madame.
Merci Madame. C'est combien?
Trente euros, Madame.
Voilà! Au revoir.
Merci Madame. Au revoir.

p 33
du thé
du café
du lait
du coca
de la limonade
du chocolat
de l'eau minérale
du jus d'orange

Et maintenant
1. *vin*
2 across. *lait*
2 down. *limonade*
3. *chocolat*
4. *café*
5. *thé*

p 35
J'ai faim, je voudrais du pain.
J'ai soif, je voudrais de la limonade.
J'ai faim, je voudrais des fruits.
J'ai faim, je voudrais des frites.
J'ai soif, je voudrais du lait.
J'ai soif, je voudrais du thé.
J'ai faim, je voudrais du fromage.
J'ai faim, je voudrais un œuf.

p 36
un café
je voudrais
sandwichs
frites
quatre
coca
limonade
jus de fruits
café

Isabelle: J'habite à Paris.
Johnny: J'habite à Strasbourg.
Charles: J'habite à Bordeaux.
Etienne: J'habite à Lille.
Farid: J'habite à Toulouse.

Laila: J'habite à Lyon.
Eva: J'habite à Nantes.
Amélie: J'habite à Cherbourg.
Jérôme: J'habite à Nice.
Marion: J'habite à Marseille.

p 44
Et maintenant
pharmacie   *boulangerie*
boucherie   *supermarché*

p 45
1. *vrai*
2. *vrai*
3. *vrai*
4. *faux*
5. *vrai*
6. *faux*
7. *faux*
8. *faux*
9. *vrai*

Et maintenant
Possible sentences are:
L'école est à côté de l'hôtel de ville.
La pâtisserie est entre l'épicerie et la librairie.
Le café est en face de la boucherie.
L'hôtel est à côté de la gare.

p 46
deuxième à droite
première à droite
allez tout droit
deuxième à gauche
troisième à droite

Et maintenant
la librairie
le café

p 48

115	*cent quinze*
321	*trois cent vingt et un*
436	*quatre cent trente-six*
159	*cent cinquante-neuf*
642	*six cent quarante-deux*
886	*huit cent quatre-vingt-six*
973	*neuf cent soixante-treize*
1325	*mille trois cent vingt-cinq*
3612	*trois mille six cent douze*
7918	*sept mille neuf cent dix-huit*
9546	*neuf mille cinq cent quarante-six*
6891	*six mille huit cent quatre-vingt-onze*
16 263	*seize mille deux cent soixante-trois*
999 999	*neuf cent quatre-vingt-dix-neuf mille*
	neuf cent quatre-vingt-dix-neuf

Et maintenant
250 000 euros
13 000 euros

p 49
Across:
2. BOUCHERIE
5. LIBRAIRIE
6. ECOLE
8. PHARMACIE
10. BANQUE
11. EPICERIE
Down:
1. HOTEL
2. BIBLIOTHEQUE
3. EGLISE
4. PISCINE
7. GARE
9. CAFE

The hidden word is SUPERMARCHE.

p 52
Et maintenant
un train

une voiture
un avion
un train
une voiture
un vélo
un bateau

p 53
Il va à Paris.
Où vas-tu, Pierre?
Je vais à Paris.

Ils vont à New York.
Où allez-vous, Jamel et Marie?
Nous allons à New York.

Je vais à Rome.

Elle va à Rome.
Où vas-tu, Fatima?
Je vais à Rome.

Nous allons à Sydney.

Elles vont à Sydney.
Où allez-vous, Sophie et Sonia?
Nous allons à Sydney.

Et maintenant
Je vais à Londres.   *Vous allez à Berlin.*
Ils/elles vont à Marseille.   *Il/elle va à Glasgow.*

p 54
Et maintenant
Tu vas à New York en avion/en bateau.
Il va à Liverpool en autocar/par le train/en voiture.

p 55
Sonia vient à l'école en autobus.
Pierre vient à l'école en autocar.
Fatima vient à l'école en voiture.
Jamel vient à l'école à pied.
Marie vient à l'école par le train.
Thierry vient à l'école à vélo.

Et maintenant

venons	*viens*
viennent	*vient*
vient	*viennent*
viens	*venez*

p 56
faux
vrai
vrai
vrai
vrai
faux
vrai

Et maintenant
Possible answers are:
Je vais à Madrid par le train.
Je vais à Tokyo en avion.
Je vais à Glasgow en bateau et en voiture.

p 58
Et maintenant
Possible answers are:
Je vais en Ecosse par le train.
Je vais aux Etats-Unis par avion.
Je vais en France en bateau.
Je vais au Japon par avion.
Je vais au pays de Galles en voiture.
Je vais en Russie en bateau et en autocar.

p 59

fille	*neuf*	*cheveux*
yeux	*verte*	*pullover*
noires	*casquette*	*tête*
père	*mère*	*coca*
je voudrais	*viande*	*frites*
gâteau	*boulangerie*	*pharmacie*
gare	*train*	